Far from All Else is the debut novel of Tom Lally. Tom is 22 years old and recently graduated from Hunter College in New York City with a degree in English Literature.

Dedicated to my family.

Tom Lally

FAR FROM ALL ELSE

AUSTIN MACAULEY PUBLISHERS™

LONDON • CAMBRIDGE • NEW YORK • SHARJAH

A CIP catalog record for this title is available from the British
Library.

ISBN 9781528902571 (Paperback)
ISBN 9781528902588 (Hardback)
ISBN 9781528957304 (ePub e-book)

www.austinmacauley.com

First Published (2019)
Austin Macauley Publishers Ltd
25 Canada Square
Canary Wharf
London
E14 5LQ

I'd like to thank Roger and Jackie Pierangelo for all of their support and encouragement.

Chapter 1

The wind blew the loose snow down the gravel path. Patches of ice scattered themselves throughout as I walked past the dormitories of Hudson Valley College which were hidden in the dark shadows of the woods. My dorm was on the other side of campus. The library and the deli, the places I usually found myself in, were the farthest places from my room.

That night, I was coming from the library having spent the past three hours typing an essay. Upstate New York felt colder than Long Island during this time of year. The dense forest with its tall trees created wind tunnels. My worn-out jeans and old sweatshirt were no match for nature.

At least it's Thursday night, I thought to myself.

I wasn't stuck in the beginning of the week, but I didn't want the weekend to arrive, where I'd sit in my room watching television and losing my mind from boredom. I wanted to drop out, but my father told me that I needed to stay for my own sake, though it was only for his benefit so he wouldn't have to deal with me. I could only come home for Thanksgiving, Christmas, and spring break. I didn't tell him I had already applied to colleges in Manhattan so I could commute next year.

I continued walking through the woods by way of the gravel path. A clay sculpture of a hand rising from the ground was erected in the middle of a fork in the path. It was out of place if you asked me. I didn't understand the meaning; therefore, I probably didn't understand why the hell I was in a place like this to begin with. A good grade point average in high school and a chance to get out of high society led me to these ivy-coated, Neo-Gothic buildings, but I wasn't ready for the difference between myself and others. The student body was diverse despite the fact that they all could have been from Brooklyn. The hipster dilemma, those who conform to others that also don't conform, yet ignore the fact that they all conform to not conforming.

Me on the other hand, I didn't knowingly conform to anybody. My hair wasn't blue. I didn't wear style hats or berets. My T-shirts didn't have any artwork or sarcastic phrases like, 'Don't look at my shirt' or 'Fuck Sting'. My ears weren't pierced. I didn't share the desires here, though I applauded them immensely. Kids who looked like the epitome of social outcasts were happy and sincere. Most didn't have a similar background to mine. They didn't like sports. They liked to talk about politics. They enjoyed embracing themselves, whether it be their sexuality or abnormal style of fashion. Everyone rolled cigarettes outside of class. I bought mine by the pack since I could barely roll without a pen to wrap the paper around. I was quiet. I didn't have a lot to say, unlike these kids who seemed happy to say what they thought. No one wanted to hear what I had to say anyway. My appearance represented someone who came from the Iowa cornfields instead of one of the richest neighborhoods on the east coast. Most were surprised when I told them where I was from and I wished their imagination was my reality, but it wasn't.

The gravel soon turned to pavement once I passed through the woods. More dormitories lined the narrow street. People flew past on their ten-speed bicycles and campus golf carts. I walked on and sucked down a cigarette quickly. I could hear music coming from one of the common rooms and people talking as the smell of burning weed lingered in the air.

Why couldn't I have that, I thought.

I knew the issue wasn't them, but me. This realization, though truthfully acknowledged, was a deep blow to my self-conscience. I didn't know how to change and I was too scared to do so anyway.

I kept my head down even though it was dark out. The wind was freezing my cheeks and the five o'clock shadow I was sporting didn't help keep the rest of my face warm. I could see the lights coming from my dorm and started to walk faster before finally reaching the door. I swiped my college ID card across the door sensor and walked through the foyer, passing the garbage cans and recycling bins that were filled with empty bottles of cheap vodka and flat beer. I walked through the second door and turned left. My room was the first one on the left. I took a deep breath and swiped my ID card again on the door sensor.

Charlie, my roommate, was lying on his bed. His dirty socks were the first thing that greeted me when I walked in. The room was dark except for a reading light that clung to the top of the pages in his book. I could see his black hair somehow lined with sweat in January. His pudgy build and glasses made him look like a marshmallow with spectacles. He wore a large T-shirt with a decal for Jumbo's Towing Company on the front. The sleeves extended down to his elbows.

"What are you reading?" I asked.

"*The Turner Diaries*," he said without looking up.

It didn't surprise me that he was reading a hard copy of a book written by a white supremacist. The book was a motivator for Timothy McVeigh when he destroyed the federal building in Oklahoma City. It was banned in public libraries and was supposedly tracked by the F.B.I. That being said, it wasn't unusual for him. I walked to my side of the room and turned on the lamp sitting on my desktop. I could see his eyes shielding themselves from the fluorescent light. He had a putrid dislike for that sort of light which he never explained, but he constantly reminded me that it didn't 'suit him'.

"You have a good night?" I asked.

"Ah. You don't really care," he mumbled.

"Something wrong?" I asked, scrunching my face in confusion.

He turned only his head and glared at me. His cheeks looked like they were packed with walnuts beneath their red dimples.

"No, nothing is wrong. I just want to read my book in peace, Jesus Christ. Turn that light off," he said.

"What the fuck is up your ass?" I snapped.

"What are you talking about, Drew?" he said and quickly sat up.

"I just asked how your night was," I said.

"Well, maybe I just want to be left alone," he said.

"Why did you go away to school then?" I asked angrily. "Cause having a roommate sort of limits your time alone."

"Why are you being a dick?" he asked.

He turned his body so his feet hung off his mattress.

"Me? I'm the dick? Are you fucking serious? I ask a polite question and you act like I just pissed all over your sheets," I said.

11

My voice was growing more agitated. I could feel my pulse echo in my throat.

"All I said was I'm reading my book and turn your light out," he said.

"How do you not understand this?" I asked.

I'd lost my temper twice in my life up to that point. Both times had been with Charlie. I hated getting angry. I lost my sense of right and wrong and just wanted to rip his head off. But Charlie just looked at me. He didn't understand. I didn't know if he couldn't grasp what I was saying or if he just had a skewed view of socializing. I sighed and cursed at myself under my breath.

"I'm sorry, I'm sorry. You didn't do anything wrong. I just snapped," I paused, "I'm sorry."

Charlie flapped his hand at me and grunted while he jumped off of his bed. He barely looked at me as he stuffed his book into his backpack and grabbed his coat from the back of his desk chair. My anger crept back quickly. I wanted to scream at him, but it wouldn't do any good except make things more awkward, though I truly thought I could yell common sense into his head.

"You know, Drew; you can be an asshole too. Don't freak out with me when you think I'm being rude. I am the way I am. That's how it is, so go fuck yourself," he said and stormed out of the room.

I should've chased after him. I wanted to slam his head against the wall. Instead, I slammed my fist on my desk which I'd been standing over the whole time. I then leaned against the slab of the wall in between my bed and desk and I looked over at the third bed in the room. Our three-person room was a two-person suite. The third person never showed up. I think he knew something I didn't. My printer sat on the blue mattress covered in Charlie's laundry for the week. Sweaty shirts and stiff stocks told me it was best to print at the library. I'd used my printer only twice this year and both of my papers smelt like leftover deli meat.

Next to the bed, near my closet, Charlie had a blown-up alien doll. It looked like a cadaver and donned a white shirt with the words, 'Beware', written in sharpie. Charlie's dad, Marv, had given it to him over Christmas break. He found it to be the funniest thing he'd seen in his life. My request to change rooms had yet to be answered. It'd been two months since I sent in my request and I'd given up hope.

My schedule gave me Fridays off. Most days, when I didn't have class, I spent watching television or playing basketball in the gym. It got harder each week to convince myself to stay. I wasn't going to do that this time. I pulled out my laptop from my backpack and placed it on my desk. I looked up Amtrak train times heading from the Hudson train station to Penn Station. The next train time was at 10:12 that night. I looked at the time in the upper right corner of the screen. It was 9:05 p.m. I could still make it if I got a cab. I'd remembered picking up a cab company's card from somewhere during orientation. I found it in my wallet, buried behind some class notes and expired metro cards. I called the number and was answered by a monotone voice.

"Taxi," the voice said.

"Can I get a cab from Hudson Valley College to the Hudson train station?" I asked.

"When?" the voice asked.

"Fifteen minutes, if that works?" I asked.

"Okay. Where you at?" the voice asked.

"McCann Hall on the south side of campus," I said.

"Okay, McCann Hall, fifteen minutes, and your name," the voice said.

"Drew," I said.

"Okay, Drew, we'll see you soon," the voice said.

"Thanks," I said.

I turned back to my computer and bought a ticket to the city. I had no idea where I was going, but I wasn't worried about that. I just couldn't be where I was any longer. I packed my clothes into my gym bag and then packed my schoolbooks and my laptop in my backpack. After searching through the desk drawers, I found my notebook which I used to write stories and journal entries in and stuffed it inside my backpack before sitting at my desk, counting the seconds until it was a full fifteen minutes from when I called the taxi. I listened to the wind swirling in the streets outside, hoping the sound would be punctuated by a car engine or a honk from its horn. The lone window's curtain was always drawn. The window was right next to a bike rack and a bench where everyone smoked. It was disconcerting to be sleeping while people could easily look through the window, so I relied on my ears to guide me. I finally thought I heard something and decided it best to leave the room. I wanted a cigarette either way.

The cab parked right in front of the building just as I crushed my cigarette on the ground.

"Drew?" the driver asked from his seat.

"Yup," I said, exhaling the remaining smoke.

"Hop in," he said.

I hurriedly jumped in and he began to drive. We drove through the narrow roads that passed the large field where rows of solar panels stood. We passed the church, a small and isolated section of the campus. It seemed strange to have it here since everyone was either an atheist or believed in anything other than God. The driver turned onto the main road that led out of the campus. We passed students walking, eliciting happiness and a sense of belonging. Their smiles and animated dances told me they were either telling a story or listening to music. I looked down at myself. My sweatshirt was ripped and the bottoms of each sleeve were burnt from trying to drunkenly light cigarettes. My sneakers were covered in dirt and paint, though I didn't remember where the latter came from. My appearance didn't matter to me. This was who I was, but nobody else seemed to like it. I liked myself sometimes, but I hated myself more often. Everyone else seemed fine and secluded in their clique, but the world swallowed me whole. I was isolated in my own self-imposed exile.

The cab ride was quiet and the driver looked tired. His eyes were bloodshot. His New York Yankees hat covered his balding, pale scalp. His denim jacket was old and worn while his knuckles looked bruised. His left hand couldn't wrap itself fully around the steering wheel. I could see him in the rear-view mirror as he licked his top gum between the gap where his two front teeth should have been.

I imagined his name was Gunner Howling, a boxer from the golden era when Muhammad Ali ruled the media and Joe Frazier stepped ahead of Ken Norton in the rankings. I could see his sculpted body and how it succumbed to the constant blows of fighting, his front teeth landing on the scorer's table where blood deflected across the paperwork like bird droppings. The cinematic end showed him in a black-and-white photo on his knees with blood dripping down his face while his competitor celebrated in the opposing corner.

He was then stuck in a dive bar in Brooklyn. He was too drunk to move and his left hand could barely hold onto the glass of water the bartender gave him to sober up. His career was gone as were his supporters. He drank away the loneliness, hoping to lose the memories of his nineteen-year-old self, shadow boxing in a Queens gym as journalists talked to his trainer about his illustrious future.

I imagined him wandering aimlessly through Bay Ridge in the cold, living in drug dens with other junkies, holding a spoon above a lit candle and wrapping a rubber tourniquet around his arm. He nearly jumped from the Brooklyn Bridge, but was stopped by a man who offered him a ride to Poughkeepsie for no reason other than friendliness. The man gave him $150 and he spent the next month sweating and vomiting away his addiction in a motel room. He then slowly worked his way farther upstate, working odd jobs trying to find the right place until one hitchhiking trip left him here. He scrounged together his remaining cash and headed to a local bar where he met the man I'd spoken to with the monotone voice. The man recognized him from his fight with Chuck Wepner in Trenton long before Wepner took Ali fifteen rounds in Ohio. He tried to hide his identity, but the scars below his eyes gave him away and he accepted it. He needed a friend. They talked about life, women, booze, wasted dreams, and unfulfilled talents. The man then brought up his cab service and his search for new drivers. A former boxer may have scoffed at the idea, but Gunner needed the money. He slept in another seedy motel when he first started working before renting an apartment above a laundromat a couple of months later. The cockroaches and cave crickets didn't bother him the way cold sidewalks and torn boots in a New York winter did. He was just happy to have a couch and four walls. Ever since, he'd been doing this.

He'd already worked a full day when we first met. He started at 5:00 a.m. and had driven all day, but only had a few fares that night. He'd eaten a gas station ham sandwich before taking a nap with his hat over his eyes. Then he got the call over his radio to pick me up. It woke him suddenly and his eyes hadn't recovered. His hand was cold and sore. He wished he had some sort of narcotic to dull the pain, but reminded himself not to think about it numerous times on our drive. He just thought about the destination and the money he would get at the end of his shift.

"We're here," he said.

"Huh?" I asked, realizing I'd spaced out.

"The train station," he pointed out of the windshield.

"Right. What do I owe you?" I asked.

"20," he said.

I pulled my wallet out from my pocket and fetched a crisp twenty and a five-dollar bill.

"Thank you," I said.

"Yes, sir. My pleasure," he said with the same resignation with which he'd said everything else.

I grabbed my bags and got out of the car. The station looked like a house. Ivy covered the brick walls and snaked through the black shudders. The entrance was through a pair of double doors. I passed through them and found the waiting room to be empty. The station clerk sat with his feet up on the desk and didn't notice me as I walked past. I grabbed a seat on a wooden bench and looked at the master clock hanging against the wall. The time read 9:38 p.m. I wanted to sleep, but I worried that I'd miss my train, so I took out my journal. I wrote reminders for myself regarding homework and college transfer applications I still needed to finish.

I started writing character notes regarding the cab driver. I went through every aspect I had come up with, jotting them down in bullets. The paper started to fill slowly with ink. As I reached the few remaining lines, a voice sounded through the intercom.

"10:12 train to Penn Station will be arriving on track 1 in fifteen minutes," the voice said.

The waiting made me crave nicotine again. I picked up my bags and walked through another pair of double doors at the rear of the building. It led me to a sky bridge covered by an iron roof. The cracked, cement floor was covered in pigeon shit. Rats ran into the shadows and through separate holes in the walls. A yellow sign declared a small segment, 'Slippery. Careful When Walking,' ignoring the rest of the hallway that was pockmarked with puddles.

I walked to the furthest stairwell where a spray-painted sign said, 'Track 1', with an arrow directing me down to the platform.

It was empty and I was glad once I saw the view. The Hudson River harbored the tracks. The darkness made it hard to see, but the soothing sound of calm waters reminded me of the beach near my house. I sat down on a bench and lit a cigarette, poorly shielding myself with my sweatshirt from the harsh wind that kicked up from the small, freezing waves as they crashed on the shore. The elements only made me unhappier and my thoughts drifted to what else was wrong in my life. College wasn't working out. I couldn't go back to my house. I didn't have a place to sleep that night. I couldn't seem to snap out of this sullen mood. I hadn't made any friends at school and I was stuck with a roommate who barely understood how to respond to "Hello".

Three cigarettes later, I was still silently measuring my life, calculating my failures against other people's successes. I didn't even notice the train approaching until the engineer sounded the horn a hundred yards from the station. I stood and picked up my bags. I walked to the yellow safety line and watched the diesel engine loudly rushing towards me. As I peered into the headlights, I started to feel my body shift. My stomach twisted, forcing me to breathe heavily. The train's headlights grew brighter and I could feel my feet moving closer and closer to the rails. As it neared within a few feet, I jumped back quickly and turned around. The wind from the passing train blew my hair forward and I started shaking. That was the first time I truly thought about killing myself.

Chapter 2
Eight Months Later

Dr. Merriweather's office was one of the few places I felt comfortable. It was small, yet inviting. It seemed as though the dimensions had been purposely set up so all of the bullshit stayed on the outside. The square room always smelt of rich mahogany and the black screens of two computers made me feel as though I had his full attention. The room couldn't have been more than twelve feet long and wide. His swivel desk chair sat next to the door while I sat on the sofa across from him. A small glass table with a chess set whose pieces were civil war soldiers and horses separated us as we went through our sessions. I'd grown accustomed to going there so the table offered itself as an ottoman to my legs, both of which seemed more lethargic than they ever should have been for a twenty-year-old.

Dr. Merriweather was in his sixties by my estimation. He had snow-white hair, but a slim figure that made his age hard to guess. It was something I didn't know if he was sensitive about so I decided it best to wait until he finally told me, though he never did.

I could hear his dogs barking whenever the doorbell rang for the next patient. His wife would occasionally peak her head through if she needed him for something important. The fact that I was in his house was even more comforting. I was in the place that most people tend to call their own, yet here he was, offering assistance to those who strayed from theirs for fifty minutes of healing.

"How do you find the medication?" Dr. Merriweather asked.

"I feel like a science experiment," I said.

"I know. We have to find the right dosage though. I know it's hard, but remember, quality of life is the most important thing. It shouldn't matter how you get there. We just need to get to that place," he said.

"I know. It's just frustrating that everyone else seems to be able to just... I don't know, to just be, if that makes sense?" I said.

I hated reminding myself that others struggled too, but they seemed to figure it out by battling the obstacles while I crumbled whenever facing something greater than my mind could handle, which seemed to be everything.

"I understand that. I don't doubt that frustration is a major part of this. But is the medication helping with the mood swings and the anxiety?" Dr. Merriweather asked.

"I guess, some days are rough, others are fine, but they, uh, they fluctuate depending on the day. I don't really know what the trigger is, but some days, I don't know, I just wake up and it feels like I'm worthless and then the next day, I feel like a normal kid again. Sometimes I sleep for fourteen hours, others I feel like I'm functioning as I should," I said.

Depression was like a game of Russian roulette. I never knew how I was going to feel. There were days when it seemed like I was just another kid navigating the potholes of adolescence as so many others did on a daily basis. Other days offered a glimpse into the world that I felt like only I could understand. Mornings would come and that feeling in the pit of my stomach would appear. No one else could creep within my head, but inside was the evidence to prove that I was completely alone in this world, the proof I only read about in articles and stories that celebrate the person that 'could've been' had they just reached out for help.

"Are you still getting sick before you go to work?" he asked.

"I was, but I finished a few days ago," I said.

"Oh right, I remember you telling me. Well, that's good," he said.

"Yeah. I just hope I feel better," I said.

"You will and I promise you'll have more energy. What else do you feel?" he asked.

"Alone. Comfortably alone. It makes it seem like just for a little while, maybe I'm not as crazy as I think I am sometimes, though I know that couldn't be further from where I'm trying to get to," I said.

"You're right. Being alone is fine, but it has to be done in moderation. Too much time alone is not good for you, similar to how being with people too much is also not good for you," Dr. Merriweather said.

"Right," I said.

I'd begun to let my head fall so I was staring directly at the faded red color of my T-shirt. Dr. Merriweather quickly understood that I wanted to tell him something.

"Go on, Drew, say it. Remember, this is a safe zone," Dr. Merriweather said.

His voice again remained calm, the result of thirty-five years of experience. It was his greatest psychological weapon. The safe confines of his office seemed to be cemented in his gentle tone. Anything I said to him would never be repeated in the outside world.

"I had another episode. I was standing on the, uh, the subway platform going to school, and I felt it again," I said.

My eyes wandered to the floor and then darted to each wall. Dr. Merriweather's degrees, encased in expensive-looking black and gold frames, reminded me that this was not something he hadn't heard before. I was not the first, nor was I ever going to be the last.

"Felt what exactly?" he asked.

"That urge again," I paused for a few seconds, "to let myself fall onto the tracks and just...let it be over."

Dr. Merriweather looked down quickly at his dress pants, as if he was slightly disappointed in himself for seeing me go through this, but his typical, relaxed manner returned within a matter of seconds.

"When's the last time that happened?" he asked.

"Happens often, a few times a week. But the urge is never there. I think that, I, uh, I think about killing myself, but I never actually feel the desire to go through with it," I said, questioning myself as to whether or not I actually had lost it all, or just felt like I had.

My chin dropped to my chest again. It seemed like my body was just reacting to my insecurities. It strangely felt as if gravity just pulled it down like bad days did to my demeanor.

"I just want to assure you again that I'm not going to do it, but it scares me that the feeling is there," I said firmly.

I didn't lie in his office. I truly didn't believe I could have ever thrown myself into oncoming traffic or a train, but the reality of feeling as though that was an option was something that not only scared me, but it made me realize that I was not okay.

"Those thoughts are not unusual for someone in your shoes. They're rogue thoughts. Your brain is almost like a pinball machine and sometimes those thoughts get trapped in between what you know and what you feel. Those thoughts might be there, but you have to combat them," he said.

His calmness allowed me to feel like I was back to being myself again, re-emerging from the dark hole of overthinking everything and anything.

"I know, but it's the thought that's frightening to me, you know? When someone asks, 'How are you doing?' I notice that I have to lie," I said.

"I know, but you can't overthink every single aspect of a conversation. The line 'how are you doing' is simply a tradition of politeness and merits an answer of 'good'," Dr. Merriweather said. "Here, that question is the basis for what we talk about, but with people outside, it isn't their business unless you want to tell them about something."

I nodded my head in understanding. I felt better when these conversations took place. It meant for a few minutes, I felt normal again. It was a high I chased, similar to the feeling a rare blunt produced when it relaxes every muscle in your body. I thought of it as the only measure of normalcy, the only hope that I would one day feel this way outside of his office, but that was something that eluded me. Safety truly was key for my sanity and I thought of Dr. Merriweather's office as the next best place to my basement where my record collection and television offered an escape from reality.

"I just want to stop thinking about it as much as I do. Music used to calm me down, but now those bad feelings kind of hover around all of the time," I said.

"Are you still writing?" he asked, scratching the shoulder of his blue sweater.

"Rarely. I have my notebooks lying around, but I kill most of my time watching T.V. or doing homework," I said. "I mess around with the guitar occasionally, but not a lot."

The truth felt good sometimes, even if it reminded me of the time I was wasting. I had been in ninth grade when I turned in my first creative writing story to my English teacher who told me that I should never give it up. That was the last person I ever showed a piece of work to except for Dr. Merriweather. Besides then, short stories and notebooks littered the dresser cabinet next to my bed. Nearly five years of writing, and I never planned on showing it to a soul.

"Playing guitar is good, but you also need to write. You cannot throw it by the wayside. You know me. I cannot tell you a lie. You have a gift. My wife read your story six times once I told her you'd written it as a freshman in high school. Have you written anything in the past few months?" Dr. Merriweather asked.

"No. I just don't think I can do it," I said.

All of my work had succumbed to the frustration of dealing with a writer's deepest fear, the question, 'Am I any good at this?' That question had driven me in different directions depending on the day. In the past six months, I crumbled into the oblivion of cigarettes and video games. Before that though, I would sit at my basement desk and write for hours on end. Both ended at the same conclusion though. I wasn't worth a shit regardless.

Dr. Merriweather shook his head and said, "Well, that's not a good way to look at it. To change you, we need to change your thinking. Write about anything you want, but know that it's not worthless. It's a part of your identity, the one you keep running away from. You'll never know until you try. I can't tell you that you'll be successful because I don't know, but I'm telling you the truth when I say if you don't try, then you'll never succeed."

"I know, I know," I mumbled.

"We have to end here today," Dr. Merriweather said.

"Okay, same time next week?" I asked.

"Yes, and do me a favor, bring something that you wrote, old or new, I don't care. I just want to see it. Is that okay with you?" he asked.

"Yeah," I nodded and laughed shyly.

I pulled a check out of my wallet and left it on the chessboard.

"Okay. I refilled your prescription; we'll keep you at two hundred milligrams for now and see how it is next week, okay? Stay strong, kiddo. We're making progress. Trust me," he said.

"I know," I said quietly though I didn't believe it. "I'll see you on Sunday."

I walked back into the waiting room where two chairs rested against the wall with a small reading table separating them. Music came from two speakers in the corners of the room, playing Mozart before transitioning into Simon and Garfunkel. The married couple waited outside as they always did. It was awkward to talk to them, as we both knew something was going poorly in each other's lives.

"How are you doing?" the man asked.

"Good," I lied, "how are you?"

"Great," they lied.

Through the lone window, I saw my dad's car parked in the street.

"Great," I said. "Have a good one."

My dad saw me walking down the cement path to the street. His Cadillac's engine started to growl a sound that I knew he enjoyed. I reached the car door and hopped in, immediately smacked by the smell of cigars and old man.

He turned around and threw his newspaper along with his reading glasses on the backseat. The gray in his hair had started to become more prominent. His face always had a stern demeanor, especially when he was driving me to and from these appointments. He was forced into this situation by my sister who pleaded with him to take me once I got back from Hudson Valley College.

He buried his face into his phone, tapping at the keys with his pointer finger like so many elderly people do. He squinted his eyes as he tried to read the small font.

"Fuckin' thing sucks," he said.

"You can turn the keyboard so it's bigger," I said.

"It's broken, fuckin' stupid ass thing," he said and threw it into the cup holder between our seats.

I sat patiently while my father put his seatbelt on, struggling to get it comfortably over his large gut that rested against the bottom of the steering wheel.

"You know he can't figure it out for you," he said.

"We've been over this. He can help me," I said.

"He's not gonna help you that much," my dad said.

"Well, it makes me feel better," I said.

"Do you really need the meds?" my dad asked.

"I think they're helping. Why?" I asked.

"Because I don't like the medication. When I was your age, we didn't have any of this shit. You made it on your own and you figured it out on your own," he said.

"Well, for me that didn't work so well," I said.

"For me, it wasn't a choice," my dad said. "Instead, now I'm paying $250 a week so you can sulk in the basement."

My dad's face became long and drawn. The withered scars of torn teenage pimples and a single spot of melanoma resided on his rotund cheeks.

He was an 'experienced' man in the sense that he hated the 'new generation'. He was thirty-five years removed from me and didn't believe in disorders or mental illnesses in his family. He was a modern Darwinist. The strong survive and the weak fail. With my other siblings, he reveled in their accolades. It made him look great. For me it was different. I'd quit basketball after my sophomore year. I'd been asked to play football after the coach saw me throwing in gym class, but I didn't want to go to practice every day. I graduated in the top 20 of my class, but I wasn't first. He looked at me like a waste of space, a human paperweight with one foot in my grave.

"You can't run from this, Drew," he said.

"I'm not trying to run from this, but it's not easy," my voice grew more distressed with each word.

"You sit in the basement all day, watching television or listening to music or doing whatever else," he stopped again. "You need to get out of the house."

"You wanted me to get a job and I did," I said.

"And then you quit, Drew! You worked for five months and then left because 'it was too stressful being a waiter'," he mocked me. "When Riley was your age, she was modeling full time. When Pierce was in college, he was interning three straight summers, going to school, and juggling that with football."

"I'm not them though," I said.

"No, you're not, obviously," he said with a short breath. "You can't hope to get better, Drew, you need to do something about it."

"I'm trying," I said.

"Trying isn't sitting in the basement. You're twenty and you still haven't gotten your fucking license," he said.

I looked over at him.

My dad rolled his eyes at me and shrugged his shoulders as if to say, 'What the fuck?'

"I always think I'm gonna kill somebody," I said. "And it's not like you're home all day. You and Grace go to the country club or to the city to see a show or you're on the boat. Riley and Pierce don't come home that often so it's not like I have someone to practice with."

"Hey, I worked hard to get where I am. I deserve time to myself. You could've learned in Drivers Ed in high school and gotten it done then like your siblings, but no, you were too busy smoking pot and writing in those silly notebooks. You wasted time and now look at where you are," he paused taking a deep breath. "I think we need some major changes, Drew."

"Like what?" I asked nervously.

"I gotta figure that out," he said.

The rest of the ride was silent. I didn't know what he meant by 'changes'. The only thing it did was scare me. I knew he already was sick of me. I was an embarrassment to him while my brother and sister were practically golden. I rested my arm on the windowsill of the passenger door and glared out as the car followed the roads of Barrington. The houses were not massive, but large. It reminded me of the town I lived in, but the aroma of wealth and snobbishness wasn't as potent. The winding roads meandered up and down hills and a few poor ten-year-olds tried to ride their bicycles on the sidewalk. We traveled past the town limits and onto Long Island's main roads passing shopping centers and fast food joints. It was only a twenty-minute ride, but I wished it lasted forever. I knew my family, along with their respective partners, was over for dinner that night.

We passed through several other neighborhoods that possessed striking similarities to each other. The houses all tended to be split-level structures where the garage rested underneath the bay window of the living room. After a few blocks, the tenant houses would make an appearance until reaching the nearby apartment complex that had two floors, but extended a full avenue. It seemed strange how the boundaries of each town worked. Houses would resemble the model for middle-class living and then over a single crosswalk, the working class homes that were classified as the lower middle-class would overtake the street. This carried on until we passed over the Long Island Railroad tracks that separated Goldencrest from Hayley's Cove.

My house belonged to the incorporated village of Goldencrest which was a part of the larger town, Hayley's Cove, though we made it abundantly clear that we were the wealthier area. Our local playground used to have one basketball court and one tennis court side by side. The town forced a law to be passed that removed the basketball court and replaced it with a second tennis court after residents filed a noise complaint. I found out later on that the complaint came from the mayor and his wife, both avid tennis players who hosted the annual Goldencrest tournament every year in May. The playground had a good set up for children. Monkey bars, four slides, a firefighter's pole, and the steel microphones to shout into, yet somehow, it was the only playground in the county without a swing set. I always wondered if this was the townspeople's feeble attempt at being different.

The feeling hit me immediately that the ride was coming to an end. The trees, although massive in height and beautiful in the way they gently rained down October leaves, overwhelmed me. The road felt narrower and narrower. It seemed like the trunks were growing closer together forcing themselves to divert the road into one single path which led straight to my front door. I had no problem with this when I knew my house was going to be empty or when it was only my sister, but when my brother and sister came back together, it meant I had to talk to the former.

I loved talking to my sister. She was the only one who seemed to like me. Riley was twenty-four and a fashion model. My brother, Pierce, was twenty-seven and a trader for Goldman Sachs. He was a former football star at Boston College.

Both made good money. Both had partners; Pierce's was soon to be his wife. Both had determination. Both had confidence. Both were functioning humans in a typical sense. It seemed as if they didn't fail. I was a twenty-year-old sophomore in college. I had worked as a waiter at a local restaurant and couldn't handle the stress. I wore ripped jeans and old sneakers every day. I lacked any thread of self-esteem, and needed to be counterbalanced by the maximum dosage of Zoloft allowable.

The only light at the end of my day was a cigarette just before I went to bed, reminding me that tomorrow was another thing to worry about, but for those two minutes, the only thing I was focused on was a single Marlboro Menthol.

We reached the gate to our house shortly. Each property on the street had an entrance gate since each house lined the water and the town didn't want people sneaking onto the beach who weren't apart of the Goldencrest Beach Club. The gate opened and my dad slowly eased the car up the driveway. The driveway had a parking space wide enough for two cars near the walkway to the front door while the rest of the path led to the garage in the backyard. I saw two cars, a Mercedes and a Jeep sitting there and immediately knew my brother and sister were at the house waiting for me.

I knew they knew where I was coming from, but I hated the hesitance on our respective parts to act as if everything was completely fine, except with Riley. I was off, possibly had always been, but it had become public information. With the exception of my sister, no one in my family understood mental illness. Instead, they feared it. They didn't know how to react because the term, 'mentally ill', suggested the idea that a noose was somewhere nearby.

As we walked up the stone steps to the front door of the house, my father grabbed me by the arm.

"Hey. That conversation stays between us. Don't go crying to Riley about this. That'll only make things worse and I'll still make those changes I mentioned," he said sternly.

I remained quiet, slowly walking forward so my father would have to release my arm, but his grasp hung firm. I felt him jerk my arm and the force pulled me back in front of him.

"Do you understand me?" he asked.

I nodded without looking at him.

"Look at me," he said, slapping my chin with his fingers.

I tilted my head towards his and nodded.

"I understand," I said before passively pulling my arm free.

27

The double doors were unlocked and I walked in first. The wood floors had been freshly cleaned. The staircase lined the wall to the right of where I stood. It led up to the balcony where I saw Grace. Her butt sat on the wood railing as she talked on her cell phone. The large bracelet on her wrist glistened against the chandelier's light hanging above the main floor entrance. Her heels were tall and her white dress pants were tight. She was a beautiful forty-five-year-old. Grace had married my father when I was fourteen, roughly a year and a half after my mother died. She'd worked as a secretary at my dad's Wall Street company in Manhattan. She didn't know much about economics, but her looks made up for what her brain lacked.

That's not to say she was dumb, but it is to say that she was merely average, and that held for everything except her appearance.

"Hey, Grace," I said.

"Hey, Drew," she said, smiling. "How was your appointment?"

"Great," I said unenthusiastically.

"Oh, that's great, sweetie," she said before turning her head back against the phone.

She talked to me like I was ten years old. I knew she didn't fully understand my dilemma. Loneliness and depression were not something she was used to and my situation made her uneasy.

"Hey, babe," my dad said.

"Weston," she said. "Come up here."

I avoided this part. The idea that my dad was with someone so supremely opposite to my mother, someone whom in my opinion, didn't hold a candle to her. Her intelligence, her diligence, her temper that could occasionally flare, her presence that was evident the second she entered a room. She never cared about money or material things. My father had always made a lot of money, but my mother still wrote at the kitchen table for hours on end.

Five books, no commercial value, still, five books, all with emotional relevance.

It was an empire of wisdom that we lost when she passed, and so to watch the man I knew who had only 'loved' a single woman in his life then grope a woman my mother wouldn't have been able to stand was bruising.

I looked at the large oval entrance to the left of the front doors. The dining room was set. The black mahogany table could seat ten comfortably. Each placemat was set with silverware, a napkin, and a small bread plate. The napkins were neatly folded as they did in the restaurant I'd worked at. It looked fancy. I knew Grace did it. She tried to be fancy, but without the wedding ring on her finger, she would be sitting behind a desk answering someone's telephones and making dinner reservations for people like my father. The set places also showed that my brother and sister, along with their respective partners, would be staying for dinner.

The kitchen was a short walk directly in front of the entrance. I walked under the balcony where I could hear chatter coming from inside. I stopped short of the kitchen, just before the wood on the floor turned into ceramic tiles and I listened to the voices of my siblings and then their partners who were accompanying them.

Riley had been with Brock for three years and Pierce with Emma since middle school. I was no longer a mystery. They were aware of my problems. I used to be the friendly and cute little sibling.

Now I was the scarred and pained youth who still hadn't experienced the hardships of being an adult.

My sneakers crunched against the kitchen floor. It smelt like chicken and noodles. I could feel everyone's eyes turn. Riley was the first to speak.

"Hey, Drew," she said and ran over to give me a hug.

Pierce and Emma followed seconds after.

"What's up, Drew?" he asked and gave me a limp handshake.

"Hi, Drew," Emma said while giving me a light, hesitant hug.

Brock came last.

"How's it going, Drew?" he asked and gave me a firm handshake.

"Hello," I replied to everybody.

I went to the refrigerator and pulled out a soda can, cracking it as I turned back to the room.

"Where were you?" Pierce asked.

"Physical therapy. My knee is killing me," I said.

I'd torn ligaments in my knee playing basketball during my sophomore year of high school. Though I acted like it was something bothersome, it hadn't affected me since the surgery corrected it that winter break four years prior. It became a paper-thin shield that everyone could see through, but I just didn't want to tell them where I'd really been.

"Yeah. I heard. What are they doing for it?" Brock asked.

"Same old exercises," I said.

"That should help," Pierce said.

"Yeah, I hope, but if you guys don't mind, I'm gonna head outside for a smoke," I said.

"That's definitely not helping you. You gotta stop that shit," Pierce said.

"Well, you know what they say, life is short, I might as well smoke up then," I said.

I could hear Pierce scoff.

I walked through the kitchen, passed the living room on the left where the fireplace and two reading chairs were. Old family photos of us when we were younger stood on the mantle next to photos of our updated family. Pierce's college football jersey and game balls were enshrined in a glass frame as were various magazine covers depicting Riley striking beautiful poses. The mirror on the wall reflected nothing but the ceiling lights above, something my mother and I used to laugh about when she was alive.

"Why did your father hang a mirror from there? What the hell are you going to see?" she used to joke with me.

The solarium was glistening with the late afternoon sun. The room, complete with two chairs, a couch, and a large television led out to the patio in the backyard. Opening the sliding door, I was immediately hit with a fresh gust of wind. The breeze came off the Long Island Sound just one hundred feet past the edge of our backyard lawn. I loved this part of the house. Summer months allowed me the pleasure of reading a book in the warm air while listening to the soft, haunting melodies of Elliott Smith and Townes Van Zandt. Fall brought a different mood, but just as serene a feel. Though slightly colder, it tended to agree with my Irish skin. The sun didn't beat down the way it did during the summer; instead, it seemed to hover distantly above the clouds.

It was close enough for me to feel and see, but far enough to avoid sunburn.

I lit a cigarette and sat on one of the reclining chairs that faced the water. The silence didn't last long; however, as I heard the back door slide open.

"You okay?" Riley asked as she slid the door closed.

She ran her fingers through her long, brown hair. She truly was beautiful. Her elegance was primed ever since she was a baby.

The modeling world was known to be cruel, but Riley had escaped without a scar. She had a perfect life. Soon to be married, wealthy, beautiful, and intelligent. People who knew her were always shocked when they met me, at least in my opinion. I knew that the rest of my family was slightly embarrassed by me, but to Riley, I was simply myself, and I forever loved her for that.

"I'm getting there," I said, holding up the cigarette.

"No, Drew, how are you doing? Actually?" she asked.

"I'm okay," I said, taking a drag.

"Sorry about Pierce and Dad. I know they're not your favorites," she said as she took a seat next to me.

"Why? It's not your fault," I said.

"I know they can be assholes on occasion," she said.

"They do have their moments," I agreed.

"How was your appointment?" she asked.

"Same old. Two hundred milligrams of Zoloft still. If it doesn't get better, then we'll try something different," I said while taking another pull from my cigarette.

"I'm sorry, Drew. I really am. I'm not gonna pretend to understand what you're going through, but I have to know something. Are you gonna call me if things get worse?" She asked.

"What do you mean?" I asked.

"I just mean if you start to feel lonely and distant. I know Dad and Grace are no help, but I'm always around no matter what," she said.

I turned to her and gave her a cheap grin.

"I will," I said.

Riley leaned over and hugged me. Her gold earrings dangled against my cheek and shoulder.

31

"God, I wish you didn't have to deal with this," she said.

"Me too, but it's getting better," I lied.

"I hope it is, Drew," she said as she pulled her face from my shoulder.

She wiped a stray tear from the corner of her eye.

"You okay?" I asked.

"Yeah, I'm good," she said, sniffling.

I gently grabbed her forearm.

"I'm gonna be fine," I said.

She grabbed my hand this time.

"I know, Drew. Are you writing?" she asked.

"Not recently, no," I said. "I thought about buying a typewriter. I don't know why, but for some reason, I think it might help me write. I love the sound the keys make."

"Are you gonna get one?" Riley asked.

"I don't know. It might be a waste," I said.

"Get one," Riley said. "It won't be a waste. Not if you use it."

The back door slid open again. It was Pierce this time.

"You guys coming in? Dinner is ready," he said, but didn't wait for an answer and closed the door.

"C'mon, let's go, Drew. I'm starving," she said.

I snubbed the nose of my cigarette in the ashtray and followed her inside.

Chapter 3

I went to the kitchen sink while everyone filed into the dining room. As I washed the cigarette smell off of my fingers, footsteps crept along the kitchen floor behind me. The refrigerator door opened and I looked behind me only to find Pierce grabbing the Britta from the shelf.

He snagged a glass from the cabinet next to the sink.

"You gonna change before we eat?" he asked.

"No, why?" I asked.

"C'mon, Drew. Look at yourself," he said, while he poured himself a glass of water.

I looked down at my clothes. My jeans were tattered and my sneakers were dirty. My messy, brown hair was uncombed and subjected to the wind. I didn't understand his problem with me wearing what I wanted within the limits of my own house.

"I think I'll take my chances," I said.

"Just trying to look out for you," Pierce said, shaking his head, "but obviously it's a waste of time."

Pierce liked to believe that his ambitions were always for the greater good of someone else, but in reality, it was what he felt was better for him. The only reason he would deride me about the way I looked was because he was embarrassed by how I dressed.

Last month, I went to the country club with him and my father for a round of golf. Pierce was so angry over how 'shitty' my polo was that he bought me six new ones from the pro shop. My father made no attempt to defend me. Instead, he simply chimed in with, "He's got a point, Drew." I guess he just hadn't noticed beforehand even though I was next to him in the passenger seat for the entire drive over. Those shirts were now rotting in the back of my closet.

"You done?" I asked.

We made brief, but solid eye contact before I left the room. I could feel his eyes following me through the walls all the way to the dining room.

Grace and my father sat at opposite ends of the table. Brock sat next to my dad, as would Pierce when he returned. Their respective partners sat next to them. I was happy to see my sister subtly wave me over to her side of the table where an open seat remained.

I sat and looked across at an empty chair. Grace had just finished making sure the table was set perfectly before returning to the kitchen to check the food. We sat around the table making small talk until Grace and Pierce returned with a platter of chicken breast bathed in some sauce I didn't know how to spell or even say. There was a bowl of peas as well as a bowl of noodles. A plate of string beans slathered in butter was placed in the center of the table. The presentation was well put together though, everything about the meal seemed very normal, despite the added ingredients Grace put in to distinguish herself as a woman with a palate.

Once everyone finally sat down, I reached into the middle of the table for the chicken breast before hearing my brother say, "Wait."

I paused with my arm stretched across the table.

"Wait until we say grace," he said.

I forgot that my dad, Grace, and Pierce were each oddly religious.

"Oops. Sorry," I said.

"Grace, would you like to say grace this time?" Pierce asked.

"Why yes, Pierce. Thank you," she said giggling.

We each grabbed each other's hands. My sister and I did it out of politeness. Brock did it because he was in his girlfriend's parents' home. My father did it because church 'saved him' after my mother passed. Pierce prayed because he considered himself something of a regional God and Emma did it strictly because Pierce did. Grace prayed because of her family upbringing. Her name wasn't Grace due to familial legacy or even its attractiveness, but for the Grace of God. She wore a cross around her neck every day and tried helping me recover my lapsed Catholicism. She and my father used to force me to church with them when I was in high school. After the six straight months of snoring in the back pew, they realized that not even God could save me.

"Oh, heavenly spirit. We thank you for the food we are about to receive as a consequence of your blessing O' Lord. To you, we thank for the nourishment of our bodies and warmness in our hearts as we all are able to be here on this lovely day. Thank you, Father. Amen," Grace finished.

"Amen," we all said in unison.

Pierce reached for the chicken first and gave a piece to everyone except me. I had to say his name six times over the table chatter before he wanted to listen. He loved that petty bullshit.

Riley immediately knew what he was doing. She quickly grabbed the noodles and dunked about half of the bowl on my plate. We quietly giggled and I shoved a forkful into my mouth so no one would see how much I had.

These dinners usually turned out the same way and this one wasn't an exception. My father and Pierce would talk business on one end of the table. Emma, Riley, and Grace would talk fashion and Riley's job on the other end of the table. Emma played with her bracelets and let her blonde hair fall from the bun she had it in before. She reminded me of a younger version of Grace. Emma had quit her job as a nurse once Pierce started making seven figures. She was going to end up like the rest of the Goldencrest wives, unemployed, uninteresting, and vaguely inebriated.

Brock politely spoke in both conversations. I wished he sat on the other end of the table. I liked him. He was a photographer from Venice, California. Riley and he met on her first large-scale photo shoot for a magazine. His wardrobe was that of an artist. His jeans were tight and rolled up at the ankles, just above a pair of brown, scuffed boots. His red-and-blue checkered flannel was tucked into his pants. His dark brown hair was neatly combed to one side and his face had pronounced stubble. I found myself jealous of his life. He was making money doing what he loved. He was happy with his life and he managed to mingle in all types of company effortlessly. He was perfect for my sister and it made me even happier for her. They were the ideal couple despite what others at the table may have valued.

I found myself stuck nearest to the women's side of the table as usual. I liked to sit next to my sister even if that meant I had to deal with listening to what the different styles of the respective seasons were. It beat listening to two grown men rifle on about the stock market, the country club, Donald Trump's appeal, and their clients, otherwise known as their 'custies'. I ate quickly. It was abnormally fast, but mentally appeasing. I knew the second I was done, I could quickly say thank you, and return to the patio for a post-dinner cigarette. Riley used to try to involve me in conversations, but she learned that I'd rather leave then feign interest.

"Thank you, Grace," I said and stood up once I finished eating.

"Wait, Drew," my father said.

"Yes?" I said.

The whole table silenced for some reason and the spotlight made me nervous.

"Pierce and I were talking. We thought you might like an internship with Paul Shapiro this summer. You remember my friend Paul, right? Either way, Pierce did it when he was your age and loved it," he said to me.

"I'm not interested in Wall Street," I said.

"Well, now, Drew, this isn't a request. You need a plan moving forward. You're currently unemployed and doing what?" he asked.

He snapped his fingers a few times as he tried to come up with the answer.

"I'm going to school," I said.

"But not working," my father continued, "and what's your next move?"

"I'm gonna find another job in the summer," I said.

"And after that, what're you gonna do? Write the great American novel?" my father asked.

"I don't know. Afterwards, I'll try my hand in writing somewhere I guess," I said.

"Drew, there's no money in writing. Mom wrote book after book and she barely made a goddamn cent," Pierce butted in.

"Money isn't my goal, Pierce," I said.

"What is then?" Pierce asked.

"Fulfillment, I guess. Happiness," I said.

My father laughed as did my brother. The rest of room sat in awkward silence.

"Will you guys leave him alone?" Riley said as she stood up.

"Drew, I will not allow my son's life to be ruined by immature values. I've already decided to tell Paul you accepted the position," my father said, ignoring my sister.

"You did what?" I asked.

"Drew, you're taking this job. I'm tired of trying to plead with you. You'll one day learn that supporting yourself is the key to happiness. Not slaving away at a career you'll never succeed in," he said.

"What the..." I was interrupted.

"End of discussion. I don't care what you have to say," he said.

The room was deathly silent and all eyes were pointed at me. I felt like I was being portrayed as the boy who couldn't grow up, and I was learning the hard way. I stared at the floor for a second. My shoulders sagged and I exhaled one defeated breath.

As I left the room, I heard my father say, "One day, you'll thank me."

I put my plate on the counter and rested my hands against its cold, marble surface. I stared at the window above the sink and my reflection appeared. For a few seconds, I daydreamed about smashing my father's face into his plate, hearing him gasp and yelp while his teeth shattered against his food.

"What the fuck?" I asked myself.

I could hear Riley arguing with Pierce and my dad.

"Why not let him do what he likes?" Riley yelled.

"Why are you always sticking up for him? He's young and naïve. He doesn't know what he should do," my dad yelled back.

"So you're just gonna tell him what to do?" she yelled.

"This will help him. He chain-smokes and hangs out in the basement all day. He doesn't do anything else," my dad said.

I left the kitchen before anyone could see me and returned to the patio. I took my cigarettes out of my pocket and lit one. The saliva in my mouth had become thicker as I tried to thwart the inevitable tears.

Our backyard extended nearly thirty yards before hitting the beach. I could see the water calmly swelling as it was pulled in by the tides. I walked on the cement that covered the perimeters of the pool and reached the lawn. A slow breeze ruffled my hair and sent embers flying from my cigarette.

The tears started to stream down my face like a waterfall. I was gargling mucus and my chest was pulsating to account for the gasping breaths I took. I walked to the edge of the lawn where the grass became sand and sat on the small ledge that looked like a mini hilltop. I sat with my legs bent and curled my arms around them. I buried my face deep inside my crumpled body and wept. It felt like I was there for hours, though it was probably only ten minutes. The cigarette I'd been holding had burned itself down to the filter though I'd only taken two pulls.

I could hear footsteps coming from behind me. I knew it was Riley immediately and didn't turn my head. She just sat next to me while I lit another cigarette.

"You okay?" she asked, folding her legs so her red shoes were wedged beneath her knees.

I nodded, wiping my nose with my hand.

"They don't know how talented you are," she said.

"I'm not. Even if I was, they wouldn't care," my voice stammered.

"You are talented, Drew. Dr. Merriweather has told you. I've told you. We aren't lying to you," she said.

"Thanks, but I don't think I can do this anymore. I can't do that internship," I said. "I'll lose my mind."

"It's still a long way's away," Riley said.

"I couldn't stop puking before I went to work as a waiter. How the hell am I gonna go to an office with people I don't know? I don't even like finance," I said.

I could feel Riley's hand rubbing my back.

"Why do I have to be the one who thinks like this?" I asked her.

"Drew, you're not alone," she said.

"It doesn't feel that way," I said.

Riley hugged me tightly, quietly hushing me while the wind blew her hair into my face.

*　*　*

The party started to leave after everyone finished eating. They had work the next morning and needed to get back to

Manhattan. Nearly an hour and fifteen minutes away by car, that meant that when 8:15 came, everybody was long gone.

Riley had a hard time saying goodbye as I walked her to the door.

"How long are you gonna be away?" I asked.

"A month at most," she said. "But don't hesitate to call."

Riley was heading to Europe for a magazine shoot. She'd gotten the call from her agent a few weeks ago. I don't think I'd ever seen her so excited.

"Don't worry about me. Go have fun. I'll be fine," I said.

"Still call. I want to know how you're doing," she said.

"I will," I said.

She hugged me tightly again. Pierce gave me a cold handshake and Emma gave me another reluctant, half-committed hug. Brock invited me to his and Riley's apartment anytime. I had been attending Redding College in Manhattan since the start of my sophomore year and hadn't once stepped foot in their apartment even though it was close to campus.

I watched as Brock's Jeep pulled out from the driveway, followed by Pierce's Mercedes as they exited through the gate. They disappeared behind the bushes lining the front of the house. I hung my head in relief and pain. One car I was happy to see leave, the other I wished hadn't.

I walked into the kitchen and found my father leaning against the island bar. Grace was standing at the kitchen sink washing dishes and dirty silverware. My father sipped scotch from his tumbler. I walked over to Grace and started helping. I could feel my father's cold stare. Grace was quiet and the uneasy feeling of undissolved tension arose.

"Drew, we need to talk," he said, sipping his scotch again.

"What about?" I asked.

I thought that maybe he'd changed his mind. Maybe he was going to apologize for what had transpired over the past few hours.

"About your psychiatrist," he said.

"What about him?" I asked.

"You're not going to see him anymore," he said.

"What?" I asked.

My body instinctively swung around so I was then facing him.

"Drew, this isn't working for me. I'm not paying some doctor to give my son medication that's not working. You don't need that psychiatry bullshit," he said.

"It's not about you," I yelled. "It's making a difference for me."

"Obviously. You don't do anything. Instead, you waste my money complaining to some douchebag in Barrington," my dad said. "I'm not doing it anymore. Cancel your next meeting, tell him thank you if you want, I don't care. I already took your medication."

"No, I need to stay on that," I said.

"No, you don't," he said.

"I need those," I yelled. "They're helping me. If you spent…"

"Don't raise your voice with me," my father interrupted. "This is my house, these are my rules, and this is my decision. Your pills are gone. I flushed them down the toilet."

I stood silently for a few seconds. I could feel the tears returning and worse yet, my father noticed them.

"What, are you gonna cry?" he asked and then walked towards me.

I remained silent but immediately stared down at my feet to avoid his anguish.

"Are you gonna cry?" he asked again.

I could see his dress loafers nearly standing on top of my sneakers.

"Look at me," he said. "Look at me!"

He slapped me across the face. The force swung my head so I was looking over my own shoulder. I slowly turned it back to my dad's glare. His eyes were fierce. They had lost their boring brown color. I swore they looked black.

"You will learn the hard way from now on. I'm tired of waiting for you. Look at you now. You look like a pussy," he said. "I'm not doing this anymore. Understand?"

I didn't speak. I just glared at his chest to avoid eye contact. He put his drink on the counter near the sink and grabbed me by my shirt. He lifted the fabric so I was standing on my toes. I grabbed his hand and he violently pulled my face towards his.

"Do you understand?" he said through gritted teeth.

"Yes," I said as the tears rolled down my cheeks.

He let go of my shirt and pushed me into the counter. He quickly chugged the remainder of his drink and started to walk out of the kitchen.

"Grace, grab your coat. We're going to the club for a drink," he said and walked away without a response.

Grace silently put the remaining plates in the dishwasher. She refused to acknowledge me and hummed as she followed my father out of the kitchen. I stood shell-shocked, waiting for the front door to close. Instead, I heard it slam a few seconds later. Then, the car engine ignited and I could hear the tires of my father's car squeal as they tore out of the driveway. I slid down the counter until I sat on the floor with my legs straight out in front of me. A tear ran down my nose before it fell to the floor.

* * *

Around 9:30, I left my house and wandered down the beach aimlessly. I found myself chain-smoking while tears continued to stroll down my face. I was glad to see that no one was on the beach. I needed to be alone. I'd finally grown tired after walking for a while and I found a trio of rocks that led out roughly twenty feet into the ocean. Higher than the tide and flat, the rocks were a perfect place to sit and let the calm waters of fall act like they could solve life's problems. I looked off into the darkness and pondered what to do next. My father's voice crept through my ears. My face didn't hurt anymore, but I couldn't get him out of my head. My heart was rushing and I momentarily paused, hoping that I would fall off of my couch and wake up. Instead, a small spray of water ricocheted of the rocks and gently landed on my face. I knew everything was real then.

Riley wouldn't be home for a month. I was being forced to become a banker. I couldn't monetarily afford to see my psychiatrist again. My medication was gone. My family either worried about me or found me a black sheep amongst the Thomas name. I grabbed another cigarette from my pocket and went to grab my lighter when a wave crashed harder than any other before had. It wasn't a giant, but nevertheless, it was a violent wave considering the past twenty minutes had just been therapeutic. The water crashed over the rocks and onto me. My feet were soaked as were my jeans. My cigarettes were ruined.

My lighter had fallen from my hand. The water had knocked loose remnants of my cigarette into my mouth.

"Come on!" I yelled at the ocean before retreating back to the beach.

I stood on the sand, shaking the water out of my hair and checking to see what damage I might have missed. I went to spit out the cigarette contents still caught under my tongue, but the wind returned. It caught my saliva and flung it back towards me, landing it perfectly centered on my shirt.

"Are you kidding me?" I asked aloud and looked around as if my audience would sympathize with me. I rubbed it off with my finger, but only managed to smudge it against my chest. I couldn't help but stare down at my sneakers. With every ounce of pressure I put on them, water would bubble through the tongue and over the laces, further dousing my sock which made that horrible 'squishing' sound.

I started to walk back towards my house. I didn't want to go home, but I didn't know what else to do except get out of those clothes. I walked for a few minutes, passing the houses that I wished I lived in, pondering a normal family life that resided within before my sneaker stepped on something. I looked down and found a glass beer bottle, broken into several, jagged pieces. The moment hit me like the wave a few minutes before. I picked up one of the pieces, examining it for a short time, but then an urge sprouted. I walked over to the shore and washed the glass to see its pointed edges. Nothing mattered to me anymore. That was something I had never felt before in my life. Liberation, to a degree at least. I turned my left-hand palms up and stared into the water, contently thinking, *This is it.*

Chapter 4

I woke up and was staring at a white ceiling. My mouth was dry and my arms felt numb. I felt too weak to lift my head. The sun shone in through the windows, hurting my eyes.

"He's waking up. Drew? Drew?" someone asked.

I saw Riley's face peer over mine.

"Where am I?" I asked through my cotton mouth.

"Oh, thank God," Riley said.

I coughed, but the dryness coating my throat made me feel like I was suffocating.

"Water," I said.

"Grace, can you grab some water please and get the doctor?" Riley asked.

I couldn't hear Grace, but I saw her quickly walk out of the room. I tried to sit up only to fall back into the pillows. I raised my hands slowly and saw that they were heavily wrapped in medical tape and mesh casting.

Goddamn it, I thought, *I couldn't even kill myself.*

"I thought you'd never wake up," Riley said and cupped her mouth.

Shortly afterward, Grace came back in with the doctor and a plastic cup full of water. Riley grabbed it and bent the straw into my mouth. I sucked until the cup was dry.

"More please," I finally said.

"Okay," Riley smiled.

I saw a tall man standing behind Riley. He politely smiled to get by her and reached the side of my bed. His hair was gray and his glasses made him look professional. He was skinny and well dressed, wearing a light blue button down and a pink tie under his lab coat.

"Hello, Drew. My name is Dr. Yates," he said.

"Hi," I mumbled.

"How are you feeling?" he asked.

"Um, I'm not sure," I said.

"Do you know why you're here?" he asked.

I stuttered and looked around at the hospital room.

"Drew?" he waited a few seconds, "Drew, you tried to kill yourself," he said.

Riley covered her face when she heard his words. I just looked at my hands.

"We were able to stop the bleeding, but you lost quite a lot of blood," he said.

"So, how long is he gonna be here?" Riley interjected.

"Well, he's going to see our psychiatrist, Dr. Phillips," he said, turning his head towards her which revealed a quarter-sized birthmark on his cheek. "Until then, Natalie here," he pointed to the thirty-something woman who stood in front of the transparent sliding door, "She's been posted to your room for your stay."

The woman smiled shyly. I sat stone-faced. Grace stood at the foot of the bed playing with her cross.

"Is she gonna be posted at the door the whole time?" Grace asked.

The doctor turned his whole body this time, "She is there to make sure Drew isn't a danger to himself or anybody else in the hospital," he politely said.

Grace nodded. I don't think she knew what to say. I didn't blame her. Mental breakdowns and suicide attempts usually didn't occur in most people's lives. Dr. Yates turned back to me.

"Now, Drew, I need you to wiggle your fingers for me. Can you do that?" he asked.

I did. I couldn't feel them but I was able to see my fingers moving back and forth.

"Okay, good," he said. "There are stitches in each wrist," he ran his finger through the air above my wrist to my forearm. "We are going to leave on the bandages until your wounds have healed in a few weeks or less. Okay? Then we'll remove the stitches."

I nodded and said, "Okay."

Dr. Yates turned his attention to the whole room, "I'll let you guys be. Let me or Natalie know if you need anything," he said and rose to his feet.

Natalie slid the door open for him and he exited the room.

"I'll be right outside if you need me," she said and slid the door closed behind her.

The rest of the room turned their attention back to me.

"Who else is here?" I asked.

"Brock just ran out to get some food. He should be back soon. Pierce is at work. He said he was coming afterward with Emma. And Dad is somewhere. Grace, do you know where he is?" Riley asked.

"Weston is at the house. He told me he was getting Drew some things," she said.

I nodded and I could feel my mood sinking like a ship. I wasn't made for this world, and somehow I was still stuck in it. My head hurt and my body ached. The blood loss had affected my entire being, but my heart still managed to spare a pulse.

"Why'd you do it, Drew?" Riley asked.

I just laid in the bed quietly. I didn't want to look at her face. I'd hurt everyone in my family, even the one person who I thought I never could.

"Drew," she said again.

Tears trickled down her cheeks. I remained quiet. Riley gently put her hand on my bandaged wrist.

"Please, talk to us," she pleaded, unable to hold her tears.

"I'm just tired right now," I said and closed my eyes.

I could hear the shuffling of Grace and Riley in the room. I didn't know what to do, so I tried to actually sleep. I wanted my head to stop pounding. I wanted my sister to stop crying. Then darkness fell over me like a blanket. I may not have been dying, but I was at least going to get the slightest bit of restful sleep.

I woke up later that night. My head felt better, but I still felt like I was too weak to move the lower half of my body. I saw Riley asleep in the chair next to my bed. Brock slept in the chair next to hers. The hospital was deathly noiseless.

I started to move to an upright position. Everything was stiff and it took me a few seconds to gain enough strength so I could sit with my back against the pillows. My shuffling woke the sleeping couple. Riley snapped awake quicker than Brock.

"Drew," she said and sprang over to the side of the bed.

The dryness had returned to my mouth. My lips stuck to my gums. Riley noticed and grabbed a plastic cup of water from the window ledge behind the chair she'd been sitting in. She bent the straw into my mouth and I finished it quickly thereafter.

"Thanks," I said.

"You just missed Pierce and Emma. Grace just left to get something to eat," she said.

A moment of silence lingered and it became obvious that my visitors were not the desired subject to talk about.

"Oh, Drew, what did you do to yourself?" she asked.

"How did I end up here?" I asked.

"Red Hollings and his wife found you. They were walking down from their house to sit on the beach. They saw you and called an ambulance," she said.

I nodded in understanding, though trying to hide my bafflement. Red Hollings and his wife nearly divorced two months ago. Apparently, Red had been sleeping with his secretary as well as the past two. He was living in his Montauk house since his wife kicked him out, at least that was the last I'd heard about him. I guessed he was back then.

How, on that special day, did they decide for a romantic night on the beach? I thought to myself.

"Why Drew? Why'd you do this?" she asked.

I paused momentarily. Brock stood up and walked to the foot of the bed.

"I, uh, I don't know," I said.

"Why did you do this to yourself?" she asked again.

I stayed silent.

"Drew, please talk to me," she pleaded.

"What do you want me to say?" I asked, "You want to hear about this shit?" I sniffled, "Why doesn't anyone just leave me alone?"

"Drew, we want to help you," she said and gestured to Brock, who nodded his head at me.

Her tears grew larger in the corners of her eyes. She looked helpless. Brock looked like a soldier returning from war, ghostly pale and worried.

"I'm sorry," I said.

I couldn't make eye contact with her.

"Look at me. Please, Drew," she said.

As Riley begged me to open myself up to her and Brock, the door slid open. My father walked in and Grace followed behind him.

"Dad? Where have you been?" Riley asked angrily.

"I had some stuff to take care of," my father said.

"Are you kidding me?" Riley asked.

"Not here," Brock said, "do it outside, but not in here. Let Drew rest."

I looked at him and nodded in appreciation. The comment quieted them, but I could see my father moving closer to me.

"What the hell you'd this for?" he asked.

I didn't respond.

"Answer me, son," he said.

Nervousness was an understatement. I felt like larva crawled through my veins and clogged the airways in my throat. I wished fear could've killed me. Then I'd be dead ten times over.

"Look at yourself. What the hell am I gonna tell everybody?" my father said.

"What are you gonna tell everybody? Are you fucking serious, Dad?" my sister shouted.

"You should be asking him that question. Look at his fucking wrists," he said.

The yelling returned and while Brock tried to make peace between the bickering, his attempt proved to be useless as I watched my family continue to banter back and forth undeterred.

Look at what you've caused, I thought.

"Alright, alright. Cut this out right now," I heard a woman's voice say amongst all of the rest. The room went quiet.

"Now, my name is Dr. Phillips. I am the psychiatrist here. If you want to scream at each other, may I suggest you go to the parking lot, but right now a young man is recovering," the voice said.

"Are you gonna be the one to solve all the problems, huh? Fucking shrinks. Fuck off, why don't you?" my dad said to her.

A tall black woman in a white lab coat and a purple sweater stood nearest the door. Her black pants were long and spotless.

"I'm gonna make this simple for each and every one of you. Leave this room right now while I have a word with Drew," she said.

Her presence was menacing. She knew how to instill fear. Her serious, brown eyes told me that she didn't want to hear any bullshit. Her brown hair with lighter highlights was left in a bob that covered her ears but didn't extend to her shoulders. It surrounded her head like a cave, only her bangs were flipped stylishly to one side.

"Ah, fuck it," my father said and stormed out.

Grace ran after him.

Riley shyly said, "Sorry," as she walked past Dr. Phillips.

The second my father spoke to Dr. Phillips; I knew she hadn't directed her anger at anyone but him. She nodded at Brock and Grace as they left the room. When the door fully closed, Dr. Phillips turned back to me. Her threatening demeanor relinquished and her face softened, revealing two healthy rows of white teeth. Her red lipstick glowed as she walked over to my bedside.

"Hello, Drew. I'm Dr. Phillips in case you didn't hear me," she said.

"I'm sorry about that. It was my fault," I said.

"The yelling?" she asked. "Please, I deal with that every day."

I smiled at her and she chuckled back.

"You're a smoker, right?" she asked.

"How'd you know?" I asked.

"Your pointer and middle finger," she pointed at them. "Skin discolorations don't look like that unless you smoke," she said.

"Oh, yeah," I said.

"Come on, Drew. Let's take a walk," she said.

She unfolded a wheelchair that had been sitting in the corner of the room and set it next to the bed.

"Where to?" I asked.

"I need a smoke," she said.

Dr. Phillips wheeled me out into the hallway. Nurses walked past and smiled while doctors filled out charts attached to clipboards.

"Where is my family?" I asked.

"I told Natalie to take them down to the cafeteria. I didn't want them to disturb any of the patients," she said.

We reached the elevator doors and she pressed the up arrow. I saw a digital clock hanging from the wall. It read 9:30 p.m.

"Where're we going?" I asked.

"To the roof," she said.

"Do you take all suicidal patients to the roof?" I asked.

"If you find a way over the fence with those hands, I'll change my routine," she said.

I laughed and I heard her do the same. She made me feel comfortable and I couldn't help but feel like I was sitting in Dr. Merriweather's office. The aura around her was interesting. One moment could show a woman whose rigor and strength lied in the grit of her teeth and the glare of those dark eyes. The next, she was simply talking without judgment.

"And no, I don't take patients to the roof, but when their family is yelling in front of them and I'm jonesing, I'll take my chances," she said.

The up arrow blinked and a loud beep followed. The doors opened and she wheeled me in. I felt the elevator climb after Dr. Phillips pressed the highest floor number before it halted suddenly. The doors opened and we were on the top floor. She pushed me passed a few rooms and nurses who didn't seem to care where we were going.

She opened a door with a sign titled, 'Roof Access'.

Upon entering, a staircase stood in front of us. The taupe walls and cracked, brown stairs led up to a red door.

"Stretch your legs," she said.

She grabbed me by my armpits and then gently pushed my back forward so I could gain enough momentum. I stood up and felt very wobbly. My legs felt weak and stiff. She held me by the arm as we walked up the steps.

"You okay?" she asked me.

"I think so. My legs feel like jelly," I said.

"That's what happens when you lose that much blood and then sleep for a day and a half," she said.

We slowly migrated our way up the stairwell and reached the door. She helped me with one hand and pushed the door open with her other. I followed her onto the black roof. My feet were cold, but it didn't bother me. I was glad I wasn't in that hospital bed anymore. We walked just outside and I propped myself up against the small, square-shaped hut where the door was situated. Dr. Phillips slid a brick it in front of the door with her foot so it couldn't close and pulled out a pack of cigarettes from her coat pocket.

"You mind Camels?" she asked.

"At this point, no, not all," I said.

Dr. Phillips held the cigarette up to my face. I grabbed it with the two fingers she'd noticed before and put it in my mouth. Then she held the lighter up to my mouth and lit the end of the cigarette.

"Thank you," I said after my first exhale.

The poisonous after burn felt so nice as it rushed down to my lungs.

"Careful none of the embers fall onto your bandages," she said.

"Okay," I said.

I flicked the cigarette, sending ash to the ground while she looked off into the dark, starless sky.

"So what happens after this?" I asked.

"What? After tonight?" she asked to which I nodded.

"I evaluate you. We see if you need psychiatric care. I've already talked to Dr. Merriweather," she said, "me and him go way back. We went to school together, believe it or not."

"Oh, wow. I didn't know," I said curiously. "So far what's your analysis?" I asked.

Dr. Phillips took a long, sweet drag from her cigarette.

"Well," she blew smoke out of the side of her mouth, "I don't think you're a danger to anyone else, but you are to yourself," she said. "I have to explore your family history, but according to Dr. Merriweather's reports, you might spend some time here with us."

I sighed and drew another pull from my cigarette.

"There's nothing worth saving here," I said.

"You know, I've heard that before, but I read one of your short stories, Drew. Dr. Merriweather sent it over to me when he heard about you. He has some pretty good things to say. I also know that your kind. I know that you, fortunately, have a pulse and a lot of years left; therefore, I came to the conclusion that there is everything worth saving, despite what you might think," she said.

She flicked her cigarette onto the ground and I did the same. We went down the same way we came up. She gently helped me make it back down the stairs and into the wheelchair. We went back down the hall, into the elevator, and back to my room. I didn't speak the whole time. I just thought about what she'd said.

What the hell did she see? I thought to myself.

We reached my room and once again, she guided me to a standing position and then onto the mattress. The sheets and pillows were nice and cold.

"Good night, Drew. I'll see you tomorrow morning," Dr. Phillips said.

"What's happening tomorrow?" I asked.

"We'll be moving you to the psychiatric wing," she said.

"How long am I gonna stay there?" I asked.

"I'm not sure yet. I'll let you know tomorrow. Goodnight," she said and left the room.

Chapter 5

I woke up to the sound of birds chirping as they flew past the window. Natalie sat in my room the entire night, watching me sleep. Though she was friendly, I found her presence to be bizarre as we barely spoke to one another.

My family had gone home. Riley felt terrible when she said goodbye. She felt even worse when I told her I was being moved to the psychiatric wing. She apologized profusely, but I understood her dilemma. She needed to go to meetings with her agent and smooth over her last-minute withdrawal from a major magazine photo shoot. I told her I would talk, but not then. I didn't want to lie, but she needed to hear something good come out of my mouth.

"Can I grab some food please?" I asked Natalie.

"Sure, I'll get someone to run in a tray," she said.

A few minutes passed before a male nurse delivered a tray of food to the room. I quickly devoured everything that sat in front me. My stomach growled with each bite and I was glad to gain back some strength.

"Oh, Drew, your dad stopped by Dr. Phillips's office earlier this morning. She updated him on your situation," she said.

"How'd that go?" I asked.

"Don't know," she said. "Only Dr. Phillips talked to him. She wants to see you in her office."

After I finished eating, Natalie wheeled me down the hall and into Dr. Phillips's office. The room looked barren like a former patient's quarters that had been converted into an office. A few paintings hung on the wall, holding images of nature and a terrified horse running through an open barn door. The bookshelf on the other side of the room contained volumes of psychiatric textbooks. Dr. Phillips sat at her desk, reading through pages that were piled in a beige folder.

"How're you doing today?" she asked.

I shrugged and held my hands up.

"Like, I, uh, like I just did this," I said.

"Fair," she said, "I have something for you."

She stood and reached down behind her desk and picked up a gym bag. It was my St. Thomas basketball gym bag from freshman year.

"Your father dropped it off," she said placing the bag on her desk.

"What's in it?" I asked.

"Clothes, I think. Your sister dropped these off last night before she left," she said and held up two cartons of cigarettes.

"She's the best," I said.

"Your father also left this," she said.

She opened her drawer and pulled out a piece of loose leaf that had been crumpled into a ball.

"He gave it to you like that?" I asked.

"He threw it at me like that," she said and handed it to me.

"Have you read it already?" I asked.

"I can't. I wouldn't regardless, but the only way I can is if you give me permission to do so," she said.

I took a deep breath and opened the ball into a full sheet of wrinkled paper. Some of the ink had stained and it looked like scotch had spilled on the header. The handwriting was messy, but I could hear every word in my father's voice.

Drew,

I am at the end of the line with you. You will live with your sister when you get out of the hospital. I WILL NOT GIVE you any money. I WILL NOT PAY for college anymore. You can use your savings for that. If you want spending money, get a job and KEEP IT. DO NOT CALL. DO NOT WRITE. YOU ARE NOT WELCOME IN THIS HOUSE ANYMORE.

Weston F. Thomas

A tear dropped onto the paper and ink slowly drained from my father's first name.

"Are you alright, Drew?" Dr. Phillips asked.

I didn't say anything. I held back the rest of my tears and leaned forward. I glided the note onto her desk. My head bobbed with an assurance that she was allowed to handle the piece of paper. She read it while I sniffled in my wheelchair.

"I'm sorry you have to deal with this," she said, putting the paper on her desk once she finished reading it.

I cupped my hands over my face.

"Drew? Drew?" she came over and leaned right next to me.

"I'm sorry," I said through my palms.

"Don't be," she said and handed me a Kleenex. "None of this is your fault, Drew. None of it."

It didn't calm me though. I wept for ten minutes before I started to tire myself out. My lips trembled uncontrollably until I was able to breathe normally again. I lifted my hands from my face and took another Kleenex from the box Dr. Phillips was holding at my side.

"Thank you," I said.

"Are you okay?" she asked.

"He hates me," I said.

"No, he doesn't. He doesn't understand you," she said.

"I don't understand me. He loathes me," I said.

"Has it always been like this?" she asked.

"Yeah, but it got worse after my mom died," I said.

"Drew, look at me," she said.

I carefully looked up and tried to relax my face, but I felt the contortions on my skin.

"You are not the reason for this. This is your father," she said.

"I am the reason for this," I said, "my dad just wants a good meal and a good shit. Anything in between, he doesn't want to hear about."

"Exactly, Drew. That is his baggage, not yours. He takes things out on you, but you are not the reason for his issues. So don't ever blame yourself," she said.

I nodded at her.

"Drew, trust me. You can't think about his problems because we can't fix them. We can only fix yours," she said. "Do you want to get better?" she asked.

"I don't know," I said.

"Then let me help you find out," she said.

Her voice held a sense of assurance combined with a degree of begging. She wanted me to become the person she thought I could be, but I didn't know whether or not we were thinking of the same person.

"The past is the past, Drew. We can't change that," she said. "But the future is unknown. You can control where it leads."

"I know," I said quietly.

"So let's work to see where you can go," she said.

"Okay," I said after a few seconds.

"Okay," she said. "We start today. I'm putting you on a twenty-one-day treatment program. We'll have a room for you at some point today."

"Okay," I said.

Dr. Phillips stayed by my side a few minutes longer and helped me settle down. I rubbed the tears away from my face, feeling the dried streams that ran down my cheeks. Afterwards, Dr. Phillips pushed my wheelchair to the door where we met Natalie, who was patiently waiting outside. She smiled and wheeled me back to my room.

I slumped in my bed for hours, awaiting the moment when I would be transferred to the psychiatric wing of the hospital. I'd seen *One Flew Over the Cuckoo's Nest* and *Girl, Interrupted*. I was expecting the worst. It was a tendency of mine to think negatively about every step, miles down the road. Experience hadn't changed my way of thinking. It'd only reinforced my fears. I feared Natalie walking back into the room. I knew her appearance would be the beginning of the unknown and I hated the unknown.

When Natalie finally entered my room, I was asleep. She woke me with a gentle nudge.

"Drew, they're ready for you," she said.

"What time is it?" I asked.

"It's almost 6:45 in the evening," she said.

I nodded and crawled out of the bed. Natalie went to grab the wheelchair.

"Do you mind if we walk? I need to wake myself up," I said.

"No, not at all," she said putting the wheelchair back in the corner.

I stood up and fixed my gown. I smelt like ocean water and sand.

"Can I shower today?" I asked.

"Yes. After we get you all set up in your room," Natalie said.

I was still weak, but I felt better than I had before, physically, that is to say. Natalie grabbed my bag from the chair next to the bed.

"Anybody call for me?" I asked.

"Uh, I don't think so. Sorry," Natalie said.

Her head looked down to the floor creating a wave with the excess skin under her chin. The bag dangled against her oval hips. The kindness in her voice faded away. She'd wanted to say yes.

"It's okay. It's not your fault," I said.

Natalie smiled and turned to hold the door for me. I slowly walked into the hallway where nurses and doctors walked back and forth checking on patients.

The walk was terrifying, to say the least. It smelled like decaying flesh and a strange combination of cough medicine and cold coffee. I felt like I was walking to purgatory, a prison for those who didn't want to live in the normal world, not because we wouldn't abide by its rules, but because we weren't capable of grasping what everyone else could. I followed Natalie's blue scrubs and the sound of her sneakers hitting the tiled floor. We walked through the hospital following the different colored lines on the floor that led the way to various concentrations. We passed doorways that read, 'Cardiology', 'Oncology', and 'Neurology'. Each was either stenciled onto the windows of the doors or printed in large red letters on the wall. Monitors chimed and patients yelled while nurses attempted to calm them down, first with pleas and then with a sedative. Doctors wheeled a crash cart passed us while an old man stretched in his doorway, slightly revealing his ass to any passerby.

Natalie led me across a skyway and I could see the street below. A paramedic team stood in a circle, laughing with each other as another team scrambled to bring a stretcher down from the backdoors of their ambulance. I thought I could see blood running down the person's face as the body shook with each twist and turn of the gurney. I could only imagine what a mess I probably looked like when they rushed me to the emergency room.

"Drew," Natalie said.

I didn't realize I'd stopped moving.

"Uh, sorry," I said still glancing through the window as I walked away from it.

We walked to the end of the hallway. Natalie opened the set of double doors by typing in a code on a dial attached to the wall. The sign above me said 'Psychiatrics'.

We went down a flight of stairs and entered an empty waiting room where the common hospital atmosphere disappeared. Rows of seats lined the walls. They were all plastic without cushions. A few pictures hung from the wall, displaying images of the building during its construction. The controlled chaos and aggressive patients yelling over the sounds of respirators and ringing telephones evaporated. I looked over at the help desk enclosed in Plexiglas.

A woman sat inside, twirling her hair and nibbling on a pen. We walked over to her. A small rectangular, opening had been carved in the window.

"I've got Drew Thomas. You guys all set with his room?" Natalie asked.

"Ah, yes, yes, we are," the woman said. She turned around to the back office door that was slightly cracked.

"Dougie," the woman said and turned back to me, "sign this please."

She handed me a clipboard with a few pieces of paper wedged tightly together. I looked at Natalie who simply nodded, urging me to complete the forms before vocally reassuring me.

"This is a standard admittance agreement," she said.

I scribbled my name on the lines where it permitted me to do so and gently slid the clipboard back through the window opening.

"Dougie," the woman behind the desk said again.

"Yes," a deep voice said.

"Can you search a new patient? Get him set up and all that?" she asked.

The office door fully opened and a man appeared. He stroked his large beard while a loop of keys jangled from his belt. I could hear them dancing against his hip with every step. He walked past the woman to a door that led into the waiting room.

"Here we are, Drew," Natalie said.

I walked in front of her and met the man at the door. He was tall and well built. His smile was calming. It lessened his

57

largeness. He lacked the swagger men his size often overwhelmed others with, but his chiseled body was noticeable through the tight shirt roped around him.

"Drew," he said, "right?"

"Yes," I said nervously.

"Name's Dougie. Nice to meet you," he said.

"Wish I could say the same," I said before quickly fixing my words. "Sorry, I didn't mean that."

Dougie chuckled to himself.

"No, it's fine. I get that a lot. Follow me please," he said.

Natalie handed me my bag.

"I'll meet you guys up there," she said and walked into the office.

Dougie led me through the hallway to a private room marked 'Storage'. There was a table with nothing on it. The bare cement room didn't even have a window. Plastic black cubbies holding transparent bins with different last names written on tape attached to the side of each surrounded us.

"I need to see your bag," he said.

I put it on the table. He opened the zippers and started digging through my clothing. He grabbed my belt and laid it on the table.

"I can't have that in here?" I asked.

"Nah, sorry, anything that can be used to hurt yourself or others. Shoelaces, strings from shorts, sweatshirts, or sweatpants, pens, hell even a nail clipper," he said.

I stood in front of him as he removed all of the strings from my clothes. He even took the shoulder strap off of my bag. He pulled out my cellphone and wallet.

"Sorry," he said, "you can't have these either."

Lastly, he pulled out a notebook. It was my spiral bound college notebook I'd used for writing, but hadn't touched in months.

"Is that a journal?" he asked.

I looked at it until my eyes were nearly on top of the book.

"Yes," I said.

I was surprised my dad had packed it. I guessed it was so he wouldn't have to see it ever again. Dougie flipped through the pages to make sure there wasn't anything stashed within it before placing it back in my gym bag.

"Okay, well, you can use a dull pencil, so I'm gonna leave it," he said.

"Thanks," I said, "I can have cigarettes, right?" I asked.

"Yes, just no matches or lighters. We'll give those to you when you need 'em," he said.

He pulled out the cartons and opened both of them. He trod his fingers across the tops of the cigarette packs. He then pulled them out one by one to make sure there was nothing hidden underneath. Afterwards, he neatly placed all of them back in their respective cartons. Dougie then turned his attention to the clothes scattered across the table. Two pairs of jeans, a few pairs of basketball shorts, five pairs of boxers, seven T-shirts, one sweatshirt, and some socks. It was everything I owned. My single pair of sneakers had left dirt stains on the surface of the table. Dougie didn't seem to mind as he started re-folding each article of clothing. His technique was great. The shirts looked better than they ever had in my drawers at home. The wrinkles in each piece of fabric from my lack of caring, however, didn't do his work justice.

"You don't have to do that," I said after he finished folding the second shirt.

"Oh, please, Drew, it's no big deal," he said.

"It's fine. Not like they are gonna get any nicer," I said.

Dougie laughed colorfully and threw his messy brown hair back with one hand. He placed the shirts in the bag and then gently laid my other clothes on top of them, still trying to be as tidy as possible. Once the gym bag was fully packed, he reached under the table and pulled out a plastic cabinet and a role of white tape. He laid the shoelaces and short strings into the cabinet, separating them so they wouldn't get tangled, along with my belt, my wallet, and my phone. He then ripped a piece of tape from its roll and wrote 'THOMAS' on it. He then stuck it on the side of the cabinet and stowed it in an empty cubby.

"Okay, now I need to make sure you don't have anything on your person," he said to me.

He pulled a small flashlight out of his back pocket.

"Okay," I said.

"Open your mouth," he said which I did, "okay, now move your tongue up… left… right… and you're good."

A few seconds passed as Dougie toyed with the flashlight, trying to fix it from periodically sputtering.

"Now, I need to ask you to do something strange. I need you to remove your gown," he said once the light remained constant.

I looked down and pointed at the lone fabric covering my body.

"I'm sorry, but I have to check," he said.

I took a deep breath and pulled my gown over my head. My wrists were the only thing covered. I put my hands over my penis.

"Drew, I need you to move your hands from your front and lift your genitals," he said.

I closed my eyes and obeyed his command.

"Okay, now turn around," he said.

I did.

"Spread your cheeks," he said.

I did. The feeling of embarrassment and shame crept over quickly. The cheeks on my face blushed. I got angry at myself.

Why couldn't I have just killed myself? I thought, *You would've never had to go through this.*

Afterwards, I followed Dougie back down the hallway and through another pair of doors that led to a single elevator shaft. Dougie pressed the up arrow button. A chime followed that signaled the elevator doors to open. Both of us silently walked in and he pressed the only other floor button which read '2'. The elevator dropped us off and Dougie led me out into another elevator waiting area. Two double doors stood a few feet from us to our left side. Dougie opened them with one of his keys.

The haunting image will never leave my head. Doors stood every eight feet or so down the long hallway. The large window at the end of hall allowed sunlight to hit the tile floor and reflect into my eyes. I was waiting for an empty wheelchair to stroll eerily out from one of the doors. Some of the patient room doors were left open. Each occupant stared if they were sitting on their bed or standing up. The others only allowed me the horror of seeing the back of their heads. I followed Dougie to the end of the hallway. It made a sharp right turn near the common room which was square shaped with a full bay window peering down to the barbed wire fence that prohibited us from sneaking out. Several patients played cards, watched television, or just sat motionless. Dougie narrated our walk, explaining what each room was. He pointed to the bathroom at the end of the hall and I could only think of what a shower might've felt like.

Putting back on the hospital gown made me feel worse. I could feel the sand and smell the aroma of seaweed pooling around my skin. Dougie started to tail off the normal beaten path. He was heading towards a door. I saw the room number, '26'.

"Here we are," Dougie said.

He pushed open the door and let me enter first. It looked like my dorm room from college. A wooden dresser had been lodged underneath the bed. An armoire, tall and made of the same wood the dresser was, sat in the far right corner of the square room. Both were that miserable off-beige color. Opposite the bed against the wall nearest the door, there was a desk. It was nothing more than an elementary school table with a surface that could hold a few books. A lonesome, dull pencil sat on the desk, perfectly placed where a right-handed person would leave their writing utensil. A tall rectangular window sat next to my bed, hovering over as it showed the pale clouds in the midst of a darkening sky. The view was obstructed by prison bars that extended across the window.

"Okay, you're all set, I think. Natalie should be on her way," Dougie said.

"Wait, she's gonna watch me still?" I asked.

"Yes. Until Dr. Phillips says not to do so," he said.

"Is she gonna watch everything?" I asked.

Dougie nodded.

"Everything?" I asked once more.

Dougie nodded again. His face echoed condolences. I turned back to my room and laid my bag on the bed. As I looked up from the plain white sheets, I noticed holes in the wall.

"What happened here?" I asked, pointing to them.

"Last patient here got a little frustrated. He took it out on the wall," Dougie said.

"What happened to him?" I asked.

"He got better. His parents picked him up this morning," Dougie said.

The holes were deep and the walls were decently thick. I immediately felt my nerves start to tremble. I wanted to break down and cry on the mattress, but Dougie couldn't leave until someone else showed up.

I took out a plain blue T-shirt and a fresh pair of jeans. I pulled out my sneakers. The tongues were lying on the heels. The lack of shoelaces made them useless.

"Is there a pair of shoes I can wear for a while?" I asked.

"You know; I think I have a pair of moccasins that've been sitting in my office for a while and no one's claimed them. They might be a little snug, but they should work," Dougie said.

"Thank you," I said and threw my sneakers onto the floor.

I could hear footsteps approaching. The squeaking of tennis shoes that I'd followed on the way here grew more pronounced as Natalie got closer.

"Hey, Natalie," Dougie said. He was leaning against the door and looked out into the hallway. Natalie appeared and walked into the room, smiling back at Dougie as she passed him.

"Natalie, can I take that shower now, please?" I asked.

"Yes, I brought you a towel," she said, raising her arm which held a blue towel folded over her elbow. "Toiletries are in here."

She opened the armoire and reached for the top shelf. A toothbrush laid with the bristles facing upwards. It was practically rubber; I guess so I couldn't hurt myself with it. Next to it was a small tube of toothpaste. A bar of soap rested in a plastic container next to a small bottle of shampoo. I noticed there wasn't a razor. I felt the stubble on my face and noticed it'd grown much sharper. I was fortunate that I liked it. I knew they weren't going to let me shave in here.

"Follow me, Drew," she said.

I grabbed my clothes and awkwardly fumbled all of my bathroom items.

"I'll grab those moccasins, Drew. They'll be in your room when you get back and, Natalie, should I bring the bag so you can change his bandages?" he asked.

"Yes, please, that'd be great, Dougie," she said.

"Thank you, mister," I said, not knowing his last name.

"Please, call me Dougie," he said and walked back down the way we'd just come.

I followed Natalie to the end of the hallway where two brown doors, marked 'Men' and 'Women' in white paint, stood. I could hear snickering from the common room and I could feel heads turning whose eyes stared at the back of my hospital gown. We walked into the bathroom and I hurriedly brushed past Natalie who was slightly surprised. One man stood at the urinal. He was wearing corduroy pants and green suede shoes. His long, blonde hair covered his neck and ended just below the collar of his black T-shirt. The shirt was one size too small and tightly fitted around his arms. He flushed just as Natalie walked in behind me.

"Oh, Harlan," she said, "I would like you to meet Drew."

Harlan turned. He had an intense face. Craters from yanked pimples and a light facial scar lined his cheeks. It looked as if he had waged a life-war and the scars were merely a reminder of what battles he lost.

"Hi, Drew. I'm Harlan," he said shyly.

He stuck his hand out. It trembled as if he didn't know what my reaction might be.

"Hi, Harlan. Nice to meet you," I said.

Harlan's grasp was slight. His palms were sweaty. I could tell he didn't know what to say next and I could see his eyes looking at my bandages.

"Well, Drew, let me show you the shower stalls," Natalie said. "Let's let Harlan get back to his room."

"Nice to meet you," I heard him say as Natalie led me past him.

"You too," I said and smiled back.

I was glad to see him chuckle in return.

There was a row of shower stalls displayed on each side of the two-person path covered in small, square tiles. The stalls were separated by floor to ceiling length dividers. I walked into the closest one. There was a small foyer where two hooks stuck out from the wall. The door also had a hook on the side facing the shower where I hung my towel. I flung my clean clothes on one of the hangers and put my soap and shampoo bottle on the small shelf beneath the shower nozzle. I went to close the door, but Natalie stopped me. She closed the stall door and stood in the foyer.

"Sorry, Drew, but I need to watch you," she said.

"What am I gonna use to kill myself in here?" I asked.

"It's part of my job," she said, "I know it sucks, but I have to."

"Please," I sighed.

"I'm really sorry," she said.

She handed me two plastic sleeves. I had to put them on in order for the stitches not to be ruined. They were uncomfortable. It felt like elastic had been wrapped around my arms. I turned around and slowly removed my gown. My embarrassment from before returned, but this time was worse. I'd never been naked in front of a girl. I faced the wall and leaned my head against it. I tried to hide my testicles and penis from her view. I scrubbed the soap around my body and let the water wash off the smell of my attempted demise. I did my best to keep my hands clear of the water sprout. The plastic wrapping made it hard to hold the soap or squeeze the shampoo bottle. I wanted to be quick, but it felt too comforting. I could feel the sand falling out of my hair and armpits.

After five minutes, I finally felt clean enough and far too embarrassed. I never once turned around to see what Natalie was looking at, but I could feel her stare every second I stood under the nozzle. I shut the water off and awkwardly walked backward into the foyer, peeling off the plastic sleeves in the process. Natalie grabbed the towel from the hook and handed it to me. I didn't even bother drying the upper half of my body. I patted the towel against my knees and thighs and dried my private parts before knotting the towel so it could hang free of my hands. I grabbed my boxers and tried to pull them without touching any of my skin. A few wet spots formed as they reached my waist. I removed the towel, revealing the red-and-white plaid underpants. I then dried my hair, torso, and back before pulling on my jeans and T-shirt. The gown that I'd thrown on the floor was gone. Natalie had it in her hands. She saw my eyes start to ponder curiously the different areas of the floor where I could have left it.

"I have your gown," she said. "You don't need it anymore."

She crumpled it into a tight ball and tossed it into a garbage can. As I tried to collect my belongings, Natalie reached for my arms.

"We need to change those," she said.

I followed her back to my room so I could drop off my toiletries. A pair of moccasins and a red medical bag sat on my desk.

"Oh, I guess Dougie brought everything already," she said to herself.

I put my things back in the armoire. Natalie sat in the desk chair and opened the bag. Her red nails pulled out a roll of heavy bandages and medical tape.

"Okay, let's see those arms," she said to me.

I held my arms out to her. She gently peeled the medical tape off of my gauze pads. Once the tape was off, she slowly pulled off the bandages that were barely hanging to my wrists anymore. It was the first time I'd seen my wounds. The cuts were shorter than I thought I'd made them. They ran a few inches upwards over the veins in my wrists which were discolored like dried fruit.

"You're lucky you didn't damage a nerve or tendon. You could've lost use in both your hands," Natalie said while she spread adhesive island cream on my right wrist.

"Quite lucky," I said.

I wished I hadn't said that. I understood the difference between being a nice guy and a dick. I lived with dicks and I felt my lonesome desirable trait was that I was friendly. That comment, in particular, made me feel like I lost some of who I was. I didn't think I ever would've said that before unless I was talking to my father or brother.

"Sorry," I said.

"Don't be," she said. "I can only imagine what you're going through. A little comment here or there is the least of my concerns. It's the rowdy ones that get me."

"Thanks," I said.

Her words made me feel better. I reminded myself that I may not have said anything like that before my accident, but I also hadn't spent any time in a psychiatric ward with faded memories of a failed suicide attempt.

"On the bright side," she smiled. "You don't need to wear those large pads anymore. The tape will work until the stitches are taken out."

"When do I get them taken out?" I asked.

"A week or so. The cuts need to heal, but you should be set soon," she said.

She ripped the final piece of tape from its original roll and pressed it against my arm.

"Okay, how does that feel?" she asked.

"Fine, I guess. I'm not really sure what you mean though," I said.

"Is it too tight or too loose?" she asked.

"Oh, no, it feels fine then," I said.

"Great," she said.

"What now?" I asked as I pulled a pack of cigarettes out from my bag and put them in my pocket.

"Well, you can meet the others in the common room. You don't have any appointments today. Dr. Phillips went home for the night. She wants to see you after breakfast tomorrow morning," she said.

Natalie led me to the common room. A couch and a couple of chairs surrounded a television set. The television sat in the middle of the room on a small, wooden table. Cobwebs hung on the corners of the open cabinet below the table platform.

I walked over to the patients sitting on the couch. One man with glasses and a shirt that didn't cover the flab protruding out of his stomach stood against the wall talking to himself as I walked past. He kept his extremities tightly pressed to his body. I thought he was crying, but I couldn't tell. He wouldn't look at me; instead, he turned to face the wall, hiding his cheeks behind his hands. I could see the sweat running through the few strands of hair he had left. I turned back to the patients sitting in the common room.

"Everyone, this is our new friend, Drew Thomas," Natalie announced. "Say hello, everyone."

I heard a few hellos. Some of them waved. The rest just stared.

"Hi," I said shyly and waved with only three fingers extended.

"Go sit down, Drew. I'll be in the office if you need me," she said.

"I thought you were watching me everywhere?" I asked.

"I'll still be watching," she pointed to the office window. Two female nurses looked up at me. Then, she pointed at two male orderlies who were roaming the hallways. Natalie's finger shifted to the ceiling. I looked up and saw cameras situated throughout the hallways and in the common room.

"I'll be around every fifteen minutes to check on you," she said.

"Okay," I said.

Natalie walked towards the nurses' station and left me standing desultory.

"What's your story?" a man on the edge of the couch nearest to me asked.

He had to be in his thirties. The five o'clock shadow on his face had a few gray strands in it. His pale, hairless skin extended down his arms and atop his head. His eyes were light blue, piercing straight to my soul like a baby's stare.

"What do you mean?" I asked.

"What you gonna tell everyone about them scars on your wrists?" he asked.

"I don't know," I said.

"Well, you better know soon. Ain't many who're gonna react well to them," he said.

I looked at his arms. They were clean. Not a single scar. He turned to the man sitting next to him who was sleeping. A blue beanie covered his eyes. Several cigarettes sat in the pocket of folded over fabric displaying a construction company logo. The man who'd been talking to me reached over and pulled five cigarettes out without waking him.

"Morgan, five cigarettes for that pack of gum," he said to a man sitting on the window ledge.

"No, Jared, I like this flavor," Morgan said, turning his attention away from the night sky.

Morgan, his name was, was holding a pack of Juicy Fruit with both hands. His eyes shifted back and forth between the gum and Jared.

"You ain't want that. You want these, I know you do," Jared said.

"I quit, Jared, remember. I don't want those," he said.

Jared stood up. His bald head was shiny. I watched him walk over to Morgan. Morgan was a young and slight man who might have been twenty-five at the oldest. He was short and skinny. Jared was a neo-Nazi look-alike with a six foot, three-inch stature. Morgan didn't have a chance.

"No one likes a quitter, Morgan," Jared said as he walked closer.

67

Morgan looked around nervously.

"That's not true, is it?" Morgan asked the rest of us.

"Look, Morgan, you know you like that sweet burn. That burn tastes better than any pack of gum. You know you like it. The calming nicotine that don't make you nervous, c'mon, Morgan, use your head," Jared said.

Jared reached him and grabbed him by the back of his neck. Morgan didn't move an inch. After a few seconds, he just nodded at him. Jared left the cigarettes next to Morgan and opened the pack of gum, shoveling a few pieces into his mouth.

"That's Jared Scherzer," someone said to me.

I turned around and found Harlan standing a few feet away.

"He thinks he's king of this place because he's the loudest one here," he said.

"What's his deal?" I asked.

"No clue," Harlan said.

"Sounds good," I said nervously.

"Never met someone like that before?" Harlan asked, gesturing towards Jared.

"No, not like that," I said.

"Welcome to the ward," he said smiling.

His voice was soft and whispery.

"How long have you been here?" I asked.

I regretted my words immediately. I lacked any knowledge of whether that question was taboo like asking a fellow prisoner what crime he was locked up for.

"Sorry, I didn't mean to say that," I quickly said.

"It's okay," he said reassuringly, "I've been here for a year and a half."

"How do you like it?" I asked.

"I mean, it's a fucking psych ward," he laughed and I joined him though I felt silly for asking such a question.

"Making friends with the newbie?" Jared asked Harlan.

I turned around and saw him standing with his arms crossed.

"Drew, this is Jared," he said.

"Nice to meet you," I said and stuck my hand out.

"The pleasure is all yours. You meetin' the king of this fuckin' jungle," he said.

He threw a few more pieces of gum in his mouth and left my hand frozen in the air.

"Okay," I said. It was the only word that came to mind.

"Okay? Shit, son, it's better than 'okay'. I own this place," he said.

I heard a voice boom out of the speakers above.

"Time for medication, everyone," a female voice said. She sounded disinterested.

The patients sitting in the common room rose and staggered to the window booth as the speaker blurted out names. Jared continued to stare at me, chomping on his gum like a handful of Red Man.

"Scherzer," the voice said.

Jared started to walk away, but continued to stare at me over his shoulder. He finally faced forward once he bumped into another patient.

"Get outta my way," he said.

"Don't worry about him. He's harmless," Harlan said to me before he walked to the office window. Names vomited out of the loudspeaker consistently, but they lacked any particular order. The nurse at the desk spoke in the same monotone voice every time.

"Thomas," she finally said.

I was the last name on the list. As I walked to the window, I filtered my eyes back and forth trying not to make eye contact, but instead wanted to simply see the faces the eyes belonged to. I reached the window where the nurse handed me two pills in a paper cup.

"What are these?" I asked.

"Zoloft. We understand that you've been taking this in the past," she said. She was a large lady. Her brown hair was knotted and poorly manicured. A mole on the side of her face made her seem frightening. It wasn't the lack of beauty that scared me. It was that she knew she wasn't beautiful, yet she also knew she was intimidating. Her hardness was cemented in her face. I wondered if that's why she was in charge of giving out medication.

"Wata?" she asked, haphazardly holding a small cup to me.

I grabbed it and splashed the pills into my mouth.

"Open," she said after I swallowed.

She leaned against the counter with her chin resting on the palm of her hand. The hair on her fingers was darker than mine.

"Move your tongue up," she paused, "down…" she paused again, "side to side," she paused once more, "move along."

She grabbed the window and slid it closed. The glass separated us then, but I didn't move. She stopped and looked at me. She raised her eyebrows that hadn't been plucked in years and shrugged her shoulders, silently telling me, 'Well, fuck off already'.

I nervously slunk off back towards the common room. The patients had returned to their same seats. The television played old cartoons. Tom and Jerry chased each other around the neighbor's yard while the bulldog slept in his shed only to be woken by a blast from Tom's double barreled shotgun. The sofa erupted with laughter every time Tom was beaten up in a hail of smoke or was crushed by a falling anvil. The balding man stuck to the wall like a fly, holding his arms as if he was cradling a baby. I was relieved to find Jared out of sight though I was anxious when I couldn't find Harlan. I didn't know who else to talk to. I scanned over the entire room. Two skinny girls wearing all black were sitting around a coffee table in the corner. I thought I could see the track marks on their arms. One had shaved the sides of her head, leaving the rest of her black hair covering her scalp. The other had long, black hair. They weren't ugly, they were ruined. I didn't know by what though. The woman with the partially shaved head ran from her seat to her room, slamming the door behind her. The other woman followed slowly behind, rolling her eyes as if she'd grown weary of being her compatriot's caretaker.

Three minutes passed and I hadn't moved. Bereavement barely begins to explain what I was experiencing. Someone didn't need to die for me to feel the way I did. I just needed to be where I was. I scoped the ceiling and the corners of the wing. The cameras offered no blind spots, at least from my limited knowledge. The hallway even had cameras positioned at either end, which allowed them to see each person coming and going from their room or the bathroom. I just wanted to be alone, completely, but this dream was dashed the second I learned of the numerous eyes in the sky. It made me nervous. I liked being invisible to the outside world, not stalked like prey in the wild.

Everyone had a story to share, similar to the first few months of college, when I tried to make friends. It meant a spotlight on all who resided within these walls, the only difference here was that the stories rarely offered any glimmer of hope. The reason you were here may have been unknown. We all stuck our hands in, attempting to grab a single shred of the truth, but whether that reason was ever revealed didn't matter. It never unearthed the pain afflicting each of us. We belonged in our mental penitentiary because we couldn't live in the world, so we went to recover at the hands of strangers who didn't know us, but had already decided, even before getting a glimpse at us, that we deserved to live.

A male orderly came up behind me.

"You okay, chief?" he asked.

"I guess," I said, staring around the room again.

"Drew Thomas, right?" he asked.

I turned and nodded at him. His wrinkles formed a smile.

"Lucius, but everyone calls me Lucky," he said and stuck his hand out.

"Nice to meet you. Why do they call you Lucky?" I asked as I shook his hand.

"Cause it's a shit ton better than Luscious," he said.

I laughed and it settled me down.

"Is there any place I can smoke here?" I asked.

"Sure, go through that door to the top of the stairs. You can smoke on the balcony," he said, pointing to a door at the end of the hallway next to the common room's white wall, "I'll go with you."

"It's fine, I'll find it. Thank you though," I said and started to walk away.

I could feel Lucky following me. I turned around after a few steps.

"Sorry, chief," he said, "but I have to watch you. Plus, I got the lighter."

"Right," I said.

The door led to an outside stairwell which was dimly lit by flickering lights. Metal fencing surrounded it the entire way down. The holes were barely wide enough to fit my fingers through.

"This for a reason?" I asked.

"Yeah. A patient jumped when this place first opened," Lucky said as I put a cigarette in my mouth. I offered him the pack, but he declined with a curt wave. He reached into his pocket and handed me a lighter. I ignited it and put the flame against the tip of my cigarette. The paper smoked and started to turn black. I handed the lighter back to Lucky.

"Now, we take further precautions with patients. I've worked in a bunch of hospitals over the years and this just might be the best I've seen," Lucky said. "You're lucky to be in such good hands."

"I guess," I said and took a pull from my cigarette. The nicotine calmed me, but it didn't cure the anxiety entirely. I still had to live in these confines and only God knew how I'd hold up. Hell, He probably didn't even know.

I returned inside afterward. The ward was oddly quiet. I hung around the common room for a little while, silently watching the *Looney Tunes*. It seemed strange that that was the show the patients decided to watch. Despite its ironic name, which amused me, I yawned repeatedly and avoided every unfamiliar face that turned to me by looking at the ground. I finally got up and went to my room.

Natalie checked on me every fifteen minutes. I could notice the constant over-watch regardless of her physical presence. My name was always in somebody's head or marked on a spreadsheet they'd need to fill out reassuring the hospital I was still breathing at a specific time. I sat in my room and laid on the bed until all patients were told to return to their rooms through the intercom. As I put on gym shorts to sleep in, Natalie came by my room again.

"Drew, I'm away. Olga will watch you through the night. I'll be back tomorrow morning," she said.

"Who's Olga?" I asked.

The woman from the medication desk appeared.

"I am," she said.

Natalie looked over her shoulder at her as they both stood in the doorway.

"I'll see you guys tomorrow," she said.

"Bye," I said.

Olga grunted loudly at her before taking the chair from under my desk and moving it into the doorway where she sat.

"You gonna watch me all night?" I asked.

"Unfortunately," she said. "People like you got me working sixteen-hour shifts."

Her tone sounded aggressive as if she wanted to punish me for complicating her shift hours. I rolled over on the bed so I faced the hole-riddled wall and touched the closest one with my fingertips. Dust and chipped paint fell onto my sheets. I stuck my closed fist through the hole. It fit perfectly. The image in my head bothered me enough to quickly pull my hand out of the hole, but I didn't want to turn back to Olga's grimace. I pulled the sheets over my head and let the darkness encapsulate me. One tear trekked down my cheek before I felt a welt in my throat. My stomach pulsated up and down like a ventilator while I trembled as my grip on the sheets got tighter.

"That's it, cry it out. That'll get you out of here," Olga said.

Chapter 6

An alarm rang from the hallway and woke me. It sounded like a fire alarm. I sat upright, letting my feet dangle off of the bed.

Olga was still sitting in the chair. She leaned her chin against her hand while her elbow rested on her thigh. Drool slithered down her lips and onto her scrubs. I stood up and changed into the jeans I'd worn the day before. Olga stirred when I sniffled. I couldn't understand how that woke her up, yet an alarm louder than a police siren didn't.

"Uh," she said, sucking the drool back into her mouth. "What time is it?"

"I don't know. Whatever time the alarm usually rings," I said.

Olga wiped her mouth. The saliva shone slightly on her pale, freckled skin. Her mole was more pronounced as her makeup wore off.

"7:30, Jesus Christ. Why can't they make it later?" she asked herself.

I slipped into the moccasins Dougie had left me and grabbed my toiletries from the armoire.

"Where you going?" Olga asked.

She was still sitting in the chair.

"Bathroom," I said.

Olga moaned as she rose to her feet. She was a few inches shorter than me, but twice as wide. A few patients with tired expressions on their faces slithered past, staring at both of us.

"Let's go," she said, ushering me with her hand to move quickly in the opposite direction of the bathroom, "C'mon. I'm hungry."

I put my toiletries on the desk and followed her. We walked down the decaying staircase to the first floor of the ward. I could hear the voices coming from the lunchroom, some of which were screaming. I ran my hand against the stairwell's metal fence that

74

barricaded us in like an old-fashioned elevator. My fingers glided against the chipped white paint, scratching a few slivers off that got caught underneath my fingernails.

"We have this so none of you jump. Kid killed himself a while back," Olga said from behind me.

She followed behind me the whole way. I could feel her hand reaching towards my shoulders whenever I walked too fast for her stumpy legs to keep up. I knew it was to make sure I didn't try to purposefully fall face down and smash my head against the stairs, but in the back of my head, I feared her hands would straddle my neck and strangle me to death. I welcomed it to some degree. It would have allowed me to leave, but I knew that if I was willingly going to die, I was going to be the deciding factor.

"Door," Olga said.

We had reached the first floor. The stairs eerily disappeared into the basement where a single light flickered and water dripped into a pre-existing puddle near the foot of the staircase. The white paint that coated the walls of the staircase abruptly stopped once one took the first step down to the basement. It was an ugly, molded brown marked by a multi-colored spray paint mural which championed itself against the wall.

As I turned to open the door, I could see a face with bulging, dark eyes screaming. The veins in his neck protruded like roots leading to a tree trunk. A quotation bubble hovered with a small arrow directed at his mouth reading 'HELP'.

"Go," Olga said. "Christ."

The lunchroom was moderately busy. Resembling a smaller version of a typical high school cafeteria, empty chairs were more prevalent than filled ones. Some patients stared at me as I passed by while others were oblivious to my presence, though I wondered what they were thinking about. I walked to the lunch line, which operated like a deli counter. Trays of food were blocked by Plexiglas so only the staff on the other side could grab them. A friendly woman handed me a tray that held all of the basics. A paper carton of lemonade, scrambled eggs, two strips of bacon, hash browns, a Styrofoam cup full of soup, a chocolate chip cookie, and dull, plastic utensils.

"Enjoy, sweetie," the woman said.

She had short blonde hair cropped in a hair net and pale skin. Her arms were skinny, but her hands maintained a gentleness when she handled the food trays. She had a fragile look, though working here probably meant she was tougher than her frame indicated.

"Thank you," I said.

I turned and stared once again at the lunchroom. I wanted to find a table that was quiet, possibly deserted, if I could. I could hear laughter and a few whimpers cascading around the room. One man ran out into the stairwell while a staff member chased after him. I sat at the first table nearest the kitchen line that was completely unoccupied. I heard Olga grunting behind me while she slurped on her coffee. She plopped down on the far end of the table. Her hair was mangled within itself. Underneath her chin were a few dark strands of hair forming a chinstrap. Her silver watch choked the skin on her wrist.

"What do you want?" she asked me.

I didn't realize that I had been scanning her every bone without discretion.

"Uh, nothing. Sorry," I said.

"Damn right, you're sorry," she said.

The eggs were nearly cold. I picked them up with a fork and let them fall back onto the plate like loose snow plummeting from a gutter. The bacon was typical cafeteria bacon, something that may have resembled pig meat, but was lightly colored and horrifically undercooked. The chocolate cookie tasted good, though I only had a bite. I wasn't hungry. Anxiety filled my stomach in the form of seemingly eternal butterflies that would only disperse once I was alone. In this place, however, being alone was impossible.

I drank my lemonade and remained quiet while Olga loudly devoured her food. I looked around at the other restless souls that wanted to be elsewhere. The two girls in black sat in the corner at the far end of the lunchroom. Another girl sat at their table in the far corner. Sitting across from the two girls was a woman shaped like a plum, wearing a blue sweater and khaki pants. I watched the girls as they stared at their food. The girl with the partially shaved head wore a plunging V-neck Iron Maiden T-shirt. Tattoos twisted around her neck like a noose, each denoting a different line of scripture though the book and lines were missing.

'If anyone curses his father or mother, he must be put to death. Beneath it read, *Slaves, submit yourself to your masters with all respect, not only to those who are good and considerate, but also those who are harsh.'*

A scar ran through the hairless side of her head. She played with the food on her plate and occasionally would glare at the woman across the table. It felt like she would scream at random, but she remained quiet, instead, grinding her teeth on top of each other. The other girl, who seemed to be the other's caretaker, sat next to her understudy. She wore a black tank top and black sleeves that wrapped around the webbing of her fingers and tightly hugged her elbows. Her eye shadow was heavy, giving her a demonic appearance. The girl sitting in the far corner caught my attention more so. She had long and vibrant dirty blonde hair. It looked relatively well kept, revealing her face to the world. She held the hair that was hanging over her shoulders like she was riding a swing set. Her knuckles went pale and she pressed the hair into her cheeks, seemingly resisting the other women's cold stares. Despite her table companions, her red long-sleeved shirt and tan skin made her seem different than the others. She seemed out of place compared to the shattered remains sitting next to her.

"You ready?" Olga said to me.

"For what?" I asked.

"Dr. Phillips wants to see you. Let's go, she wants you in at 8:00," she said.

I stood up while Olga grabbed the strips of bacon off of my plate and shoveled them into her mouth. She started to walk back to the door we'd entered. On the way, she dumped my tray into a garbage can. I followed silently behind, still looking around the room. Harlan was sitting at a table near the door. We made eye contact and nodded our heads at each other, though we each lacked a smile. He sat with the others I'd been with the night before, including Jared whose plate was overloaded with food while the others' plates, except for Harlan's, were missing items.

"Goddamn it, shut up when I'm talkin'," Jared said to one of the patients.

The patients went silent. Harlan sat with his head down, casually ignoring Jared's desire for attention. Courageous, at least it seemed, I wondered why he didn't fear Jared the way others seemed to.

Olga led me back to the staircase, letting me walk in front of her again. I looked back at the mural on the wall. It seemed to fit every situation in this place perfectly. I felt as though I belonged on that faded, crippling cement, screaming alone in the dark while others passed me by without the faintest notion of what I was going through.

We went back to the second floor and walked through the main corridor. Roughly halfway down, Olga grabbed my shoulder and turned me so I was facing a door. Stenciled across the door's chest was Dr. Marilyn Phillips, M.D. Olga knocked. I heard shuffling coming from inside, the stacking of papers and the sound of feet dropping themselves from the desktop. I could see Olga's bloodshot eyes rolling up towards her eyebrows as the time on her watch ticked away. We might have waited thirty seconds or so, but Olga was as impatient as a famished dog. The knob finally turned and Dr. Phillips appeared, wearing a white lab coat over a gray suit.

"Morning, Drew. Thank you, Olga," she said.

"My pleasure. Natalie will be back to check on you when she gets in Drew. I'll see you tomorrow Dr. Phillips," Olga smiled and turned around. I imagined her smile quickly faded once her back was facing us.

"Come in," Dr. Phillips said.

I entered the room behind her.

"I thought your office was on the other side of the hospital?" I asked.

"That's the department office I use. I'd rather not bring people here. It can be uncomfortable for those who haven't seen it before," she said.

The room was wide. The barred windows let the early morning sunlight creep over her desk so her shadow loomed larger than her actual size. Filing cabinets lined the wall along with more pictures of the hospital's construction from the early 1900s until the final product in which we were sitting in.

"How was your first day?" she asked me.

"Uh, different, I guess is the best way to put it," I said.

"Different is one way to put it, but are you comfortable?" Dr. Phillips asked politely.

"I mean, I'm fine. It just seems strange answering hospitality questions in a psychiatric ward. And I don't mean to be rude by saying that," I said.

"No offense taken, but do you have any questions regarding your stay?" she asked.

"How long am I gonna be on suicide watch?" I asked.

"Until we feel that you are no longer a risk to yourself," she said.

"When does that happen?" I asked.

"When you progress into a better state through our therapy sessions, medication, and group activities. For this to work, you need to participate though. I always have people trying to cheat the system, but if you accept the system, you'll get out of here sooner," she said firmly. "I'm not trying to be rude or accusing you of anything. I'm just telling you how it is."

"No offense taken," I said. "When do I start the therapy sessions?"

"Started a few seconds ago," she said looking at the clock that hung above the doorframe. I turned to see it before facing forward again. I smirked at her and she did the same back.

"How are your supervisors? They told you the rules they follow, right? Fifteen-minute check-ups, bathroom monitoring, the camera system, cigarette breaks, all that?" she asked.

"Yes, I've been told. The supervisors are fine. Olga seems to like me a whole lot," I said.

"She likes everyone a whole lot. Don't mind her. She's a good nurse in terms of enforcing the rules, but let me handle the emotional side. If she gives you trouble, just let me know. She's a good woman, but age catches up with you and I think that's true for her more than it is for most," Dr. Phillips said.

"What happens now?" I asked.

"Now, we talk. How do you feel?" she asked.

"My hands are sore," I said.

"They will be for a little while," she said. "Within a week, the cuts should start to feel better."

I stared down at my hands. I rolled them over and back so they were facing right side up again. They were pale and the medical tape made them look like an offensive lineman's hands on Sunday. My hands along with Dr. Phillips's office made me uneasy. I never thought I'd be sitting in a psychiatric ward under suicide watch. Every aspect started to sink in as my eyes rolled around the room. It felt like the night before had been a dream, but then it cemented itself in reality. I was a psychiatric ward patient.

I tucked my fingers over one another, tightly pressing my thumb against them so the skin turned white as I thought about smoking a cigarette. Dr. Phillips noticed when I started grabbing my lips with my free hand after a few seconds of silence.

"Jonesing?" she asked.

I nodded. She pulled out her pack of cigarettes and slid it across the desk.

"You sure I can smoke in here?" I asked before picking them up.

"I do," she said.

I lifted a cigarette from the carton before pushing the pack back to her. She tossed a book of matches to me. I folded the flap over the match and ripped it out against the matchbox.

"Why do you light it that way?" Dr. Phillips asked.

"What do you mean?" I said as I slid the matchbook across her desk.

"Why do you fold it over like that and tear at it?" she asked, pointing at the match I fanned myself with in order to expunge.

"Just learned it that way, I guess," I said.

"You seem angry when you do it," she said.

"I'm not sure how I feel right now," I said.

"How so?" she asked.

I took a long drag from my cigarette and exhaled the smoke through my nose.

"I'm in a mental ward with scars on my wrist because I tried to kill myself, and yet I'm still here," I pointed to the floor, "My own father disowned me through a letter. I continue to hurt my family, and yet again, I'm still here," I said as I put the cigarette back in my mouth.

"Yes, you are here," she said. "And we're going to try to get you out of here."

"What if I don't want to be here," I said and twirled my index finger to encompass the planet.

"I'm going to show you that you deserve to and should be out there," Dr. Phillips said and pointed at the window.

Chapter 7

I was walking back from Dr. Phillip's office, past the common room and the man who leaned against the wall without looking at anybody. Lucky was talking to him, trying to get him to watch television. Music lightly sounded from one the patient rooms. I followed it to a slightly cracked door and peered inside.

I saw Harlan sitting on the edge of his bed, strumming an acoustic guitar. His hand glided through the riff and I started to hear the melody he was playing. It was Audioslave's *'Be Yourself'*. I watched while he played until I accidentally touched the door with my hand. The wood frame creaked against the rusty metal hinges. Harlan's face turned quickly to the door and he stopped playing.

"Hello?" he said.

"Uh, hi, Harlan," I said pushing the door open.

"How long you been out there?" he asked.

"A couple of seconds," I said. "Sorry, I didn't mean to intrude."

"No worries, kind of stupid to think I can play and be left alone in this place," he said, smiling as he did so. "Come in."

I walked into his room and sat on the chair that jutted out from beneath his desk. I wondered if I was allowed to be in another patient's room, though I would soon find out when Natalie came to check on me.

"They let you have that in here?" I asked and pointed at the guitar.

"It's from the arts and crafts room, so I have to ask when I want to play it and then give it back when I'm done," he said.

"Gotcha. Song sounds great," I said.

"You like that song?" He asked.

"Yeah, I have a record collection back home, well, sort of home, I guess. I got a few Soundgarden records and *'Out of Exile'* a while back," I said. "I like Chris Cornell's voice."

Harlan's eyes grew calmer. He smiled at me. It felt like a certain wall fell between us and instead of being two patients in a mental ward, we were just two guys bullshitting about music.

"Yeah, he might be my favorite singer. You play at all?" Harlan asked me and held out the guitar to emphasize his question.

"I dabble. I mess around with it when I'm bored, but I only learned a few songs," I said.

"Which ones?" Harlan asked.

"I'm not really good at any of 'em," I said.

Harlan laughed quietly and my nerves settled around him. Social interaction made me nervous, but for some reason I felt calmer than I usually would have. My mind wasn't racing nor were my hands trembling. I was reacting like a normal person.

"I know what you mean. I didn't have a television or computer, so I had to teach myself from the radio," he said. "It took me six months to learn the basic chords."

"No television or computer?" I questioned, "I don't think I would have been able to cope," I said, trying to laugh.

"As if I did?" he questioned me, motioning his head around the room, inaudibly saying, "Look at where we are."

I sat silently, stumbling over the next few words. I grunted, incensed at what I had just said until I could hear a small crackle of laughter.

"I'm just messing around," he said while a cheeky grin crept across his face.

"I really didn't mean that," I said smiling back to him.

"It's fine. Sorry for scaring you, it's just nice to finally talk to someone who, I guess, I dunno, is okay," he said.

I could hear in his voice his dislike for what he was saying and I understood. Some of the other patients had serious issues that made them difficult to be around and the number of possible friends one could make was small.

"I get it," I reassured him.

Harlan's door suddenly swung open, shocking Harlan so he dropped his guitar pick. Jared peeked his head through.

"What the hell you two doing?" he asked loudly. "We playin' cards, gents. Both of ya's are playin'."

His shaved head matched with the gray strands of his five o'clock shadow gave him a domineering stature. I stood up and was about to walk towards the common room. I expected Harlan to follow me, but he remained seated. I stopped in my tracks as he locked eyes with Jared. The tension that boiled felt like watching steam funnel over a pot lid.

"Not today, Jared," Harlan said.

"Well, why the hell not?" Jared asked.

"Because we don't want to," Harlan said.

"We? We? You want me to play asshole with them assholes?" Jared asked.

"I guess so," Harlan said whilst nodding.

"Motherfuckas," Jared said.

He slammed the door. The doorknob raddled in its socket and we could hear Jared angrily bad mouthing us to the patients inside.

"Those two assholes, Harlan and that newbie, ain't playin'," he yelled.

Harlan shook his head.

"You're not scared of him?" I asked.

"Who? Jared? Nah. I've been here awhile. He's only been here six months. All of his shit gets old," Harlan said.

He returned to the guitar, fumbling through the bed sheets to find his pick.

"He seems a little dangerous," I said.

"Nah, he's fine," Harlan said.

"How do you know that?" I asked.

"Because he's here with us. He could very well be a sociopath or whatever, but the dangerous ones they move up to the farms and others, well, they get locked up," Harlan said.

"So why is everyone else afraid of him?" I asked.

"Because Jared is loud. He feels this 'jungle', as he calls it, is his property. Most of the people in here don't have the ability to combat someone like that, so they simply obey," he said as he continued to sift through his bed sheets. "Ah, there you are." Harlan pulled the guitar pick out from beneath the fabric and gracefully slid it across the strings so it played a note.

"How long you think he's gonna be in here?" I asked.

"I got no clue. He could get moved if he keeps being the way he is, but I think he will be in an institution for the rest of his life," Harlan said.

"Sorry, I don't mean to pick your brain on this, but why do you think he'll always be institutionalized?" I asked.

"There are rumors about him. His uncle is Charles Manson. I've heard stories about him bare-knuckle boxing. I've even heard his parents found dissected cats in his room. I heard another one saying he tied a dog's collar to a train and let it drag behind," Harlan said.

"Jesus," I said. "How the hell are you not scared of him?"

"Cause they're just rumors," Harlan said.

"Who told you them?" I asked.

"Jared," he said with a smile on his face.

He strummed another note and I took a seat where I had been prior.

"How are your wrists?" Harlan asked.

"Uh, good, I guess," I said.

"Weird question, right?" he asked.

"I'm just not used to it yet," I said.

"I'm not trying to be a dick when I say this, but you might never get used to it," Harlan said.

"Yeah, I think I'm there already," I said.

"Same thing happened when I first got here," Harlan said. "I tried to drive my dad's car off a cliff. They said it was a miracle I survived. I think it was because I was so relaxed, my body didn't get as banged up as it should've. My dad's pickup though, that's another story," Harlan finished with a chuckle.

"I'm sorry," I said.

"It's not all bad, I guess," he said.

"How so?" I asked.

"Destroyed my dad's baby," he said.

"Not a fan of him?" I asked.

"Who? My dad? No, not one bit," he said.

The conversation started to weld itself into a familiar direction. I didn't want to question him on something so personal, but his shattered familial relationship made me feel like I wasn't alone. My dad's letter ran through my head like bowling ball dispenser, each word creeping through just slowly enough for my spine to quiver as I heard his voice screaming at me.

"I wish I could've ruined something of my dad's," I said.

"Not a fan?" he asked.

I shook my head.

"What was wrong with your dad," I asked, "if you don't mind me asking?"

"He was a mean son of a bitch. I dunno, me and him never got along," he said.

"I'm sorry," I said.

"Thanks," he said.

His characterization didn't affect him as much as it did me. Harlan scratched his arms and pulled the collar of his T-shirt down as he turned back to the guitar. I didn't like how forward I'd been, inquiring about his daddy issues, but his words left me feeling a strange form of kinship.

"How about your dad?" Harlan asked.

"Cruel bastard. He never liked me much either, hell he fuckin' disowned me yesterday," I said.

I didn't like divulging this information, but I couldn't regress. It was something about Harlan, a weird aura that functioned like a bank vault. Anything I said was just part of the conversation.

"Then you got something out of it too," Harlan said.

"How so?" I asked.

"You'll never have to see that cruel bastard again," he said.

I smiled at him and chuckled through my nose. I hadn't thought about it that way.

"How'd you get those scars?" he asked.

"Nothing to tell really. I found some broken glass on the beach and then, you know," I said and held up my arms to show him the medical tape. "And then I woke up in the hospital."

"Were you looking for the hospital or the morgue?" he asked.

"I wasn't hoping to wake up in a hospital bed," I said. "Why do you ask?"

"I get curious sometimes. Some people try to be put here. It's like a vacation away from their troubles. Others want their troubles to be gone entirely," he said.

"How can you tell the difference?" I asked.

"The scars," he said.

"How do you mean?" I asked.

"Across the wrist means the hospital. Up the arm means the morgue," he said.

I swallowed the air that was in my mouth and darted my eyes away from his.

"Sorry," Harlan said. "I get carried away. I just haven't had a conversation like this in a while." His voice grew quiet, though it felt like I could hear him screaming at himself in his head.

"It's fine, really, no worries about it all," I assured him, "I'm just, you know, new to it, I guess."

"You don't have to tell me. I didn't mean to put you on the spot," Harlan said and paused for a few seconds. "You wanna play?"

A change in conversation lingered like the smell of cigarette smoke, but a segue evaded us. Harlan held out the guitar to me with the strap dangling behind it.

"It's fine, I don't really play too often. I like listening more," I said and waved my hands hesitantly.

"Come on, Drew. I'm not judging, just loosen up a bit," he said.

I smiled. Once again, he seemed to be correct. Harlan might have been all of twenty-three, but he seemed like the old man in your neighborhood. Quiet and wise, as if he had seen it all, from storming the beaches at Normandy to the Beatles arriving in America, to JFK getting shot, to reaching the moon, to the end of the Vietnam War, and so on.

"Okay," I said.

I grabbed the guitar from his hands and placed the strap around my shoulder.

"Here you go," Harlan said with his hand extended, holding the pick in his palm.

"Thanks," I said.

It felt strange holding the instrument. My wrists hurt from the odd angle I took to hold the guitar. I sat back in the chair and let the guitar rest on my knee.

"Play something," Harlan said.

I chuckled with anxiety and took a deep breath in an effort to calm myself. I started by hitting the first note, three strums downward, onto the 'g', up, down, up, down, down, and so on until the song repeated itself.

"Wonderwall," Harlan said after the first few notes.

I nodded my head and stopped playing. A smile emerged across my face.

"I thought you said you couldn't play that well?" he questioned me.

"I mean I can play a few things, but I can't do anything outside of a few chords and easy songs," I said.

"So what? Doesn't mean you can't play," he said. "What other stuff do you know?"

And so we played guitar for the next thirty minutes and I felt better. Natalie checked up on me, but only poked her head through the door and waved. I wanted to thank her for just letting us be. It was a kind gesture that allowed me to forget about my predicament and simply relax. Harlan tried to teach me some basic power chords, the southern rock noises that audibly allowed you to envision Memphis to New Orleans, and the blues. He played Howlin' Wolf and Chuck Berry, almost to perfection, at least to my ears. His hands glided effortlessly up and down the strings like a moth perching itself towards the light from a window. Smooth barely seemed like a fair word to describe his ability. It was harrowing. I leaned back in the chair and just watched him. Then he'd give the guitar back to me and try teaching me the notes that would allow me to play every song, little tricks along with a capo to make the strings sound crisper.

"Drew," I finally heard Natalie say over the music.

She stood in the doorway and Harlan stopped playing.

"Sorry to interrupt, but you have a visitor," she said. "Morning, Harlan."

"Morning," he said.

"Who is it?" I asked.

I was confident it was my sister, but if it were my brother or father, I wanted to be prepared.

"I don't know. They just told me you have a visitor," she said.

"Okay," I said and turned back to Harlan, "I'm gonna see who this is. I'll be up in a bit."

"I'll be here," he said.

Natalie guided me to the stairs.

"Where are we going?" I asked.

"Visiting room," Natalie said.

Chapter 8

The visiting room looked like it had once been a cafeteria. Lunch tables were lined up with stools welded onto the bottom bars. The corners of the room had chairs decorated with flowers, others with stripes. There were a few other patients in the room. Some I'd never seen while others I'd seen in the common room the night before.

"She's right there," Natalie said. Her finger pointed to a table in the center of the room where a woman sat wearing jeans and a sweatshirt with a pair of running sneakers on her feet. She turned her head and smiled. It was Riley. I walked over to her while Natalie silently wandered her way to the corner where she could watch me interact. Riley stood up and ran over to me. Her arms tightly wound themselves around my back and I could hear her trying to control her weeping by resting her head on my shoulder.

"I'm so happy to see you," she said.

"Here I am," I said.

"I'm sorry I missed you yesterday," she said.

"It's fine. I was sleeping for most of the day anyway," I said.

Riley slowly began to regain her composure. She finally released me so we were both looking at each other.

"You look like shit," I said.

"Yeah, you look like a star yourself," Riley said back.

We laughed together and it eased the sadness brooding over us like a thunderstorm.

"Let's sit," I said.

We walked over to one of the lunch tables and sat on opposite sides.

"How're you doing?" Riley asked.

"I don't know," I said.

"Stupid question," Riley said.

I scratched my wrist where the medical tape had annoyed my pale, Irish skin and left a red indentation.

"Why, Drew? Why'd you do it?" she asked.

I shrugged. I clenched my jawbones and held my lower lip outward so I had an under-bite.

"Drew, please talk to me," Riley pleaded.

"What do you want me to say?" I asked.

"Anything, just give me something," she said.

"Just felt bad, I guess," I said.

"What happened that night? Why didn't you call?" she asked.

I sat on my stool, my hands holding my chin with my elbows placed on the table. I tried not to look at my sister. Instead, I found a spot on the table, possibly a coffee stain, and studied it. Riley then placed her hand on top of it.

"Drew, please. You're scaring us," she said.

"Us?" I asked.

"Yes, your family, Me, Pierce, Dad, Brock..." she tried to continue.

"Don't tell me Dad cares about me. I got his fucking letter," I snapped at her.

"What letter?" Riley asked.

"He didn't tell you?" I asked.

"Tell me what?" she asked.

"He told me never to come back. He said I'm supposed to live with you when I get out of here. If I get out of here that is," I said.

Riley leaned back. Her facial expression told me that she was bewildered by the news. I think that she was even more crushed than I was.

"How?" she stuttered, "When, when did you find this out?" she asked.

"Yesterday when I was getting moved into the psychiatric wing," I said.

I didn't like my father, but there is something about the personal hatred of my own kin that bothered me. I thought about my brother when he was my age. Only a sophomore, he managed to start the final six games for Boston College's football team. My dad used to take me and my sister to some of the home games that were played on early Saturday afternoons. My dad was the loudest parent there, reminding every spectator that number 19 was his son, the great Pierce Thomas. I looked at Riley and thought of her. My dad was so proud to produce a model that he overlooked the other characteristics that made her Riley Thomas. It was her picture on magazine covers and billboards that made her important to him.

"Don't worry about him, Drew. You know you can stay with me and Brock," she said.

"I know, but still, it hurts when..." I tried to say, but this time, I wasn't able to contain myself. I leaned my head on the table and covered it my hands. I could feel the other patients and their visitors looking at me. Riley ran around the table to my side. She patted my hair and rubbed my shoulder.

"It's okay, Drew, it's okay," she said.

Riley seemed lost for words. I felt worse knowing I once again managed to hurt my sister. Her relationship with my father would be destroyed over this. My dad had never been cruel to any of my siblings, but Riley wasn't like Pierce. She thought like our mother. Her gift didn't lie within her beauty, but within her emotional intelligence. I never wanted to be the one to cripple her relationship with my father through my issues with him or his issues with me.

"Drew, please look at me," she said. "Please, Drew. Please."

I let my hands sink back to the table. I sniffled and rubbed my face with my forearms before I finally looked at her.

"Dad never understood you and you know what? He doesn't deserve to. You do what you have to do in there and when you're ready, you can live with me and Brock," Riley said.

"You want to ask Brock first?" I asked.

"He'll understand. I asked him if I could come alone today. He understands," she said.

I wanted to question her. The way I turned out forced me to question everything. The only pictures flashing through my head were Riley and Brock fighting about how they wanted to get married and start a family, not raise the family black sheep who they'd have to explain to their biological children.

"I don't want to be a burden," I said.

"Drew, you're never a burden. You're family," Riley said.

"I'm a time bomb," I said.

"Don't think about everyone else," Riley said, "Think about you. You need to help yourself. Brock, Pierce, me, Dad, whoever, it doesn't matter. All that matters right now is how you're feeling. Brock and I will be here every step of the way."

I smiled at her, silently wondering how she could be so kind. I was lucky to have her by my side, but I felt I didn't deserve it.

"Sorry about ruining your shoot," I said.

"Don't be. It's just a job," Riley said.

Anger in my stomach brewed as I realized my attempt at eluding my inner problems only exacerbated them. I was the reason Riley had to give up her upcoming job and lose payment as well.

"No! No!" I said and slammed my hands against the table. The vibrations hurt my wrists and I squealed in agony. I felt Riley grab my arms by their skinny biceps.

"Drew, stop, stop, please," she begged.

"I'm so sorry," I said.

"Don't apologize," she said.

"I ruined it. I know how bad you wanted that," I said.

"Drew, I will never put work over family," she said. "You are more important than getting photographed."

"Did you tell them what happened?" I asked.

"No, I called my agent and told them I had a family emergency, but I didn't go into specifics. I didn't know if you wanted anyone to know," she said.

I sulked with my head staring into my lap. I almost didn't know how to react anymore. Feeling this way had become commonplace and I felt I had extinguished every expression of emotional turmoil.

"Tell them," I said.

"But, Drew…" she said.

"Please, tell them. Don't hide this if it affects your career," I said.

"Drew, it won't affect…" Riley tried to say, but I cut her off again.

"It's not an excuse. It's the truth. Don't keep my secrets if it affects you," I said. "Please don't do that."

Riley sat back in her chair. The sadness seemed to recede and the gaze on her face became something different, like she was looking at our mother.

"You are a good soul, Drew," she said as she leaned over me and kissed me on the top of my head. "You are truly unlike the rest of us."

"I know," I said. "Most of us aren't locked in psychiatric wards."

I perked my head towards her slightly, exhibiting a crooked grin with only my lips. Riley saw me and laughed. We embraced for a while, though there wasn't a doubt in either of our minds that it might be too long. It simply was and that made it better.

"Drew, please promise me you are going to try and get better," she said.

I thought for a few seconds before answering.

"I don't know if I can promise that," I said.

"You have to promise me," Riley said seriously. "I know you might not see it, but I do. I cannot lose you. You're unique, not broken."

"I feel broken," I said.

"So try to fix yourself," she said.

"How?" I asked quickly. "Someone please explain this remedy that is so goddamn easy."

"By promising me," she said. "You're worried about hurting others, well, the more you hurt yourself the more pain we, me and you, are going to experience. So promise me."

I turned my body so that I was looking directly into her light blue eyes. They let my mind wander, but never allowed me to escape the harshness of reality. I thought about what she said and hated her for it initially. She'd given me a reason to live.

"I promise," I said.

Chapter 9

Natalie took me back upstairs after an hour or so in the visiting room. Riley found it hard to say goodbye, but I reassured her that I would keep my promise. That silenced her worries though it percolated mine. While Natalie followed behind me as I walked up the stairs, passed the flickering lights and cracked cement, I could only think about two words I said to my sister.

"I promise," I said quietly to myself.

I could see my sister's face cropped in permanent resolution that this was the only way she felt I could get better. I grew angry and felt she was being selfish, using her relationship with me as an antidote to suicidal ideations and crippling anxiety, then I realized I was behaving like a child internally. We reached the door to the second floor and I heard chaos echoing through the hallways of the wing. Someone was crying and others were yelling at each other. My feet momentarily stopped and Natalie accidentally walked into me. I guessed she had been pre-occupied by making sure I didn't try to nosedive to the ground below.

"Are you alright?" she asked.

I didn't respond before she quickly perked her ears to the bedlam ensuing in the following room. She peered through the small window located at eye level on the door.

"Jared is at it again, I think. I can't really see too well," she said.

"Fighting?" I asked.

"No. He's just going on another one of his rants," Natalie opened the door and said simultaneously. "It's fine. He does this sometimes."

For some reason, I didn't believe her. I thought her composure was something learned, not natural. Learned through years of experience and work at state hospitals before people started to find electrocuting a person's temples for being a 'nuisance' morally wrong. I didn't have a choice though. There wasn't a second door or even an air vent to crawl through. Natalie's presence forced her words to be a command, despite the lack of authority in her voice.

We entered the corridor and looked down the long hallway where I could see Jared standing on the couch in the common room. Someone was crying, maybe even two people were, but the sounds cluttered together like freight yard racket only told me that I shouldn't have walked through that door. I stopped dead in my tracks again.

"Drew, you'll be okay," she said from behind me.

I took one deep breath and nearly toppled over during my first step. I'd forgotten how to walk amidst the commotion. The toes of my moccasins kept hitting the floor first, sending my body weight forward before I could catch myself with the toe of my other shoe. I decided simply to take short steps, barely lifting my feet from the ground.

"Newbie," I heard Jared say.

I looked up from the floor and saw his evil eyes looking into mine.

"Yeah, you," Jared said. "Motherfucka' told me he don't want to play no cards."

The louder he got, the worse his speech became. I saw Dr. Phillips standing in the common room behind the couch Jared was using as a podium.

"Where's Harlan at?" he yelled as he scanned the crowd and found Harlan poking his head out from his room.

"Ain't gonna play cards today, huh? How 'bout tomorrow? You gonna come to your senses, cause the rest of these jokers ain't playing now neither," Jared said.

Harlan looked at him bleakly before closing his door. Jared grew more agitated. He jumped off the couch and started to walk to Harlan's door.

"What're you gonna do, Jared?" Dr. Phillips asked.

"Whatever I want," he said as he tried to walk past her.

"You gonna yell at him some more?" she asked.

"Get outta my way," Jared said.

He lifted his hand to intimidate the smaller Dr. Phillips, but she didn't move. I didn't even see her blink. Her hands remained firmly gripping her hips.

"You touch me and there'll be consequences," she said.

"Whatchu gonna do?" he asked.

"Have it your way," she said. "Alright then, to the yellow room."

Dougie and Lucky both appeared next to Jared. They'd been standing in the common room, but my view was blocked by the walls of the ward and the other patients who cowered similarly to myself. Dr. Phillips stepped away from Jared while a nurse I'd never seen before wheeled a gurney with unbelted restraints clinking against the rails. All three of them wore small masks over their mouths and noses, blue scrubs over their bodies, and rubber gloves.

"Don't touch me," Jared said.

He lifted his fists as the two men approached. Dougie and Lucky surrounded him near the wall. Dougie lunged first, grabbing Jared by the arm. Lucky quickly grabbed the other. Jared tried to fling them off, swinging his body violently. Both men held their grip tightly as the veins in Jared's neck grew more noticeable with every grunt he made. The unknown nurse guided the gurney closer to them while a trio of other nurses whom I'd also never seen before, all dressed in their protection outfits, appeared. They all grabbed a separate part of Jared while Dougie and Lucky took either halves of his body. They managed to lift him onto the gurney and wrap the restraints around his arms and legs. His squirming rattled the metal rails viciously.

"I have the needle," one of the nurses said as she walked around her coworkers who continued to hold Jared's extremities.

"Got him?" the nurse asked once she stood next to his shoulder.

"Yeah, we're good," Dougie said for everyone.

The nurse swiped a small patch across Jared's arm, coloring the small area of skin red.

"Don't put that in my fuckin' arm," Jared yelled as the nurse bent down.

She guided the syringe into his arm before announcing, "Shot's in."

His movements ceased after a few seconds and the nurses each released him. Some of them pulled their mask straps from behind their ears as they stepped away from the gurney while Lucky and Dougie started to wheel it down the hall. Harlan had re-opened his door and was leaning against the frame. I walked over to him while Natalie went to Dougie and Lucky's side.

"That ever happen before?" I asked him.

"Yeah, occasionally. He loses it sometimes when he feels he isn't being worshipped," Harlan said.

"What is the yellow room?" I asked.

"It's a room down the hall covered in yellow padding. The walls, the ceiling, the door, even the floor is covered in yellow cushions. They put people in there sometimes when they're hurting themselves or going to hurt somebody else," Harlan said.

He looked at the other patients in the ward who were having difficulty returning to their prior activity and then darted his eyes to Jared being wheeled away. Someone turned on the television while Dr. Phillips sat with a patient who'd been crying.

"Is he okay?" I asked Harlan and pointed at the man sitting with Dr. Phillips.

"Sammy? Yeah, he's okay. He's a good guy, but he's fragile. Jared freaks him out sometimes and he needs to be calmed down," he said.

"When is he gonna get back?" I asked.

"Who? Jared? A few hours probably," he said. "How was your visitor? If you don't mind me asking?"

"It was good," I said.

"Who was it?" he asked.

"My sister," I said.

"How is she taking this?" he asked.

"Like a tornado in Manhattan. She's worried, but she's keeping it together, at least she seems like she is," I said.

"People shouldn't be un-phased by something like this," Harlan said. "Those that don't are people who deserve to be in here more than us."

"I think I know a few of those people," I said.

"I bet I know a few more," Harlan said.

"Okay, everyone, group time," Dr. Phillips said to all of the patients.

Harlan and I walked into the common room where Dr. Phillips stood in the center. She turned chairs around and placed them in a circle.

"Everyone take a seat please. Sorry about that, but everything is okay now," she said.

Dr. Phillips smiled at each one of us as we walked to our chairs. Maybe two people returned their smiles to her, the rest of us kept our faces flat and emotionless or just stared at the floor to avoid eye contact with anyone else. I counted fifteen patients sitting in the circle. The gothic girls sat next to one another. Harlan and I sat next to one another while Sammy walked over to Harlan and sat next to him.

"Sammy, this is Drew," Harlan said.

"Hello," I said. "Nice to meet you."

I extended my hand across Harlan's lap space.

"Th-the pl-pl-plea-pleasure is mi-mi-mi-ne. I'm-I'm-I'm Sammy. It's gre-gre-great to me-me-meet you," he said nervously.

His hand grasped mine, but our handshake was agitated by a tremor running down Sammy's arm.

"You too," I said.

Dr. Phillips sat at the head of the circle. She faced everyone with her back to the hallway. I saw Dougie and Lucky wheeling back the empty gurney along with Natalie who walked with her arms folded by their side. They all walked past the common room and rolled the stretcher into a closet in the hallway.

"Drew," I heard someone say.

"Yes," I turned my head quickly.

"Over here," Dr. Phillips said with a chuckle.

"Sorry," I said.

"It's fine. Now I would like you to introduce yourself to the others if you haven't already done so," she said.

I looked around at the room. Heads were strangely incoherent in their mannerisms. A few people looked at me, but I tried to avoid eye contact with them for longer than a second. Some stared at the ground or rattled their heads like a lantern swaying in someone's hand.

"It's okay, Drew, stand up," Dr. Phillips said.

And so I did. It wasn't graceful. It was robotic.

"Uh, hello. My name is Drew Thomas. Nice to meet everyone," I said.

A few people waved, the rest sat motionless and silent.

"Everyone say hello to Drew. It's his first day of group therapy," Dr. Phillips said.

They all complied though most didn't make eye contact. The united 'hello' sounded like gibberish with a few patients entering once the rest had finished. I sat down again.

"We are happy to have you," Dr. Phillips said. "I'm going to read the groups for today."

Everyone sat around half listening except for me. I was nervous about what group therapy might entail. I'd seen movies and shows where there is a talent show or you have to spill your guts to people you've never met before. I didn't think that I could take that, not then at least.

"Okay, in the first group which will meet right here with me is Drew, Sammy, Leighton, Otis, and Isaac," Dr. Phillips said.

I stopped listening afterward. I'd heard my name and while I was less unnerved when hearing Dr. Phillips was going to be the group's therapist; it didn't fully quell my nervousness.

"Drew, you okay?" I heard another voice say.

I looked up at Harlan who was standing in front of me.

"Drew?" he asked me again.

"Yeah, sorry. Daydreaming," I said.

"I'm with Natalie in the art room so I'll see you later," Harlan said.

"Okay, I'll see you later," I said.

I watched him walk away, skinny arms flailing at his sides. His fragile body motions made him seem like he was looking for a light switch in a darkened room. I heard the scattering of chairs sliding against the floor and the clapping of shoes against it echoed as people walked to their assigned meeting rooms. I remained seated while Dr. Phillips started moving some of the chairs out of the way so we could make a small, tight circle.

"Gather around everyone," she said to us.

Sammy had been sitting in the same spot. He and I moved our seats closer to Dr. Phillips so we could see the light freckles below her eyes. I was surprised by the smoothness of her skin that made up her cleavage. She didn't have a single noticeable wrinkle or sunspot. It was a soft surface that looked something like the fresh top of chocolate pudding from a cup. Her figure was well maintained as well. She was slightly round, but only so that she looked heavenly real to the eye. Her features were not overly impressive, but when combined, she looked great.

Sammy continued to slide his chair to make the circle tight, but he accidentally pushed his chair too far and stopped with his legs almost fully intertwined with mine. I nearly tumbled over as Sammy's large elbow dug into my ribs. I turned my attention to him and looked at his Velcro sneakers that were nearly two times the size of my moccasins.

"I'm sor-sor-sorry, I did-did-didn't mean-mean-mean to-to-to. Oh go-go-god, are you o-o-okay? I'm sor-sorry, I swear-swear-swear I did-did-didn't mean-mean-mean to," Sammy begged me to understand.

He backed himself away quickly while his hands started to shake.

"I know. It's fine, Sammy, really. Don't worry about it," I said truthfully.

"Bu-bu-bu-bu-but," Sammy repeated with loud gasps.

"Sammy, it really is okay," I said.

I didn't know how to react, but thankfully Dr. Phillips heard everything and rushed over.

"Sammy," she said as she kneeled in front of him, "Sammy, He's fine, you're fine, and he's not angry with you."

Something in her voice made Sammy relax. He simmered down quickly and smiled at her. His big, blue eyes looked like a tarsier's behind his spectacles. Horn-rimmed with particles accumulated in the corners, I couldn't tell if he was crying or not.

"O-o-o-o-okay, Dr.-Dr.-Dr. Phil-Phillips, I'm sor-sor-sorry," he said.

He let his neck dangle again so only the top of his head was facing Dr. Phillips.

"Why are you sorry, Sammy? You didn't do anything wrong," Dr. Phillips assured him.

"Bu-bu-but, I-I-I don't wa-want peep-people to be ang-ang-ang-angry wi-wi-with me," Sammy muttered.

"And they're not. No one is," she said.

"Are you-you-you su-su-sure?" Sammy asked.

"I'm positive," she said. "Can you look up for us?"

Sammy lifted his head upwards and his big, blue eyes returned.

"There you are," Dr. Phillips said with a smile. "It's okay, Sammy. Trust me, it's okay."

"O-o-okay," he said.

Dr. Phillips returned to her seat and everyone else continued their uninterested behavior. My reaction was that of a newcomer, eyes wide and rapid head movements to see if others were as affected as I was. The only faces I saw, though, were ones who were speechlessly questioning why I was reacting the way I did.

When Dr. Phillips finally sat down and looked at all of us, she noticed my uneasiness. I guess it must have been palpable because she nodded her head at me which I believed to mean 'Everything is okay. Relax and we'll talk later'.

With this, I calmed myself and watched Sammy as he wiped his eyes and sucked the snot back into his nose.

"Okay, today we are going to talk about your ordeals," Dr. Phillips said bluntly. "I think that we should tackle this problem head-on. I think we should show Drew the importance of sharing and listening to others. Drew, please do not be shy. This is a safe place, so do not be alarmed, but if you wish not to participate, you may do so. Sharing is not mandatory."

I nodded at her. She then said, "Secondly, I want to add, Drew, that everyone here struggles with something, whatever it might be. The reason we group you the way we do is to help hone in the idea that you are not alone and others can provide support. You will eventually be grouped with everybody in the following days. We try to make this as comfortable as possible."

I nodded my head again. I wondered if this is what a rookie felt like in the clubhouse before opening day or a prisoner walking through the gates while he gets heckled by hardened inmates.

"Who wants to go first?" Dr. Phillips asked. "Sammy? How about you start today?"

I looked over at Sammy. He was sweating through the greasy hair that flopped across his forehead. His hands shook against his thighs while his right foot started to tap against the floor.

"Uh, I, uh, I, um, o-o-okay," he said."

"Great, Sammy," Dr. Phillips said. "Please go ahead."

Sammy leaned forward from his seat so he sat with perfect posture. But the second he wanted to speak, he hunched forward again so the top of his head was all we could see. His hands clung to each other, intertwined like gothic tree branches. His knuckles turned white as he tried tearing through the skin between his fingers. I stopped watching. I didn't want to watch his hands shatter as a result of nervousness. I wanted to cover my ears so I wouldn't hear the crack followed by Sammy's screams. The thought made me quiver and I found my hands grappling with each other while I tried to stop them, but like magnets, they started to align and I hoped that Sammy would have a quick speech.

"Well, I-I-I don't-don't know how to-to s-s-s-ay this," he mumbled, "I-I-I-I do-do-don't know why-why I-I-I have-have depr-depre-depre-depression."

"Why do you think you feel the way you do?" Dr. Phillips asked.

"I-I-I gue-guess it's becau-becau, oh duh-duh-damn, because I ha-ha-have anx-anxiety all the-the ti-ti-time," he said.

"Why do you think you have anxiety all of the time?" Dr. Phillips asked.

"I-I-I-I thi-ink my-my-my da-dad ha-ha-ha-ha-had some-some-some-something to do wi-with tha-that," Sammy said. "He u-use-used to be-be-be-beat me and my-my-my momma ev-ev-every duh-duh-day."

"Sammy, breathe, you're safe here," she said.

Sammy looked slightly more relaxed after a few moments of breathing through his nose and out of his partially opened mouth.

"I-I, uh, I-I th-think, it, it was be-be-because he ha-ha-hates me," he said. "Every-ery sin-sin-single thi-thin-thing I di-di-did was wro-wrong. Now, I-I-I thin-thin-think every-every-th-thing I-I-I d-do is-is-wro-wrong."

"Sammy, thank you for being so brave. Can anyone relate to what Sammy is saying?" Dr. Phillips asked.

"I guess I can," a girl said.

I was able to surmise that she was Leighton from the fact she was the only female in the group. I recognized her immediately the moment I saw her red, long-sleeved shirt. She was the girl I'd seen sitting with the two gothic girls in the cafeteria. She sat with her legs crossed. Her gray slippers and baggy plaid pajamas were an interesting look as she was someone who without makeup would still shock those around her. Her shirt tightly wrapped around her body, displaying a healthily skinny frame.

"Okay, Leighton, please share," Dr. Phillips said.

"I mean, my foster-parents visit me every week now, but until they took me in, I bumped my way through foster homes for a while. The other 'parents'," she raised her fingers to show quotation marks, "liked to beat up everyone. I had one home where she used to take the girls and he used to take the boys. He would put the boys in dresses if they did something wrong and the girls would be sent to school in the boys' unwashed clothing that was too big. It hid the welts from the paddle she used on us, or the rope she'd rub on our chests to burn off the skin. I don't think I ever got over that. I guess that not's hard to tell being that I'm here," she said and the room laughed. "But I know what Sammy means. You end up judging yourself through the eyes of others who hate you and then someone tells you that life is worth living. For me, it didn't feel that way."

I listened intently to her every word and occasionally glanced at her, hoping to get a clear image without openly staring. She had a slightly raspy voice with a gravelly tone that made her seem experienced, maybe even damaged, but it worked for her. Her face was beautiful, holding light hazel eyes and a button nose. Her face looked comforting and her smile was nurturing. She looked at the entire room and never once seemed nervous to speak about her ordeals though I wondered if she was doing so on purpose to hide from other tragedies she didn't want to talk about. Either way, I envied her ability to face what she'd been through.

"Does this way of thinking still occur for you, Leighton?" Dr. Phillips.

"Well, I guess so, in a way. I made decisions that were strictly out of hatred for myself based on their hatred of me. That's why I'm here. I still struggle with it now, but I know or at least think that they were cruel, but—" Leighton said.

"I don't think that you should think about them being cruel as a question," a man said.

I looked over to the man sitting next to Dr. Phillips. His dark skin was tainted by red pulsing bumps and chipped teeth that were rotting. His eyes were bloodshot and derelict. He constantly rubbed his arms as he waited for the subtle moments to pass while Dr. Phillips wrote something down on her clipboard. I saw the blemishes upon his arms and neck where dead veins resided.

"Why is that, Otis?" Dr. Phillips asked.

"Because they were cruel," he said.

"I understand it in context, but it doesn't change the way I feel about it. I don't know why," Leighton said.

"That's not uncommon," Dr. Phillips interjected. "Child development is heavily influenced by parental figures and the nurture given to you as well as the environment you grew up in."

"Yeah, but it isn't that easy," Leighton said while scratching the sleeves on her arms.

"I know. It's a process. You are getting there, but these things take time," Dr. Phillips said.

"Otis, would you like to share anything else?" Dr. Phillips asked.

"Same shit keeps happening to me all the time," he said.

The beard he donned was poorly manicured and patchy. His face seemed sucked dry by grief. His hoodie, which was missing its two strings, was thrown over his scalp, but his long dreadlocks were still visible around his neck.

"I hear voices in my head and see things that shouldn't be there," he said.

"What do you see or hear?" Dr. Phillips asked.

"I see this man with a loud voice. He screams at me that I'm gonna die before I turn twenty-five. He said the same thing before I turned twenty-one. He shows up in my room at night. He's a large guy. He's always holding a lantern and it lights up his face. His eyes are holes in his head and his eyebrows and mouth are made of wire. He always says I'm gonna die or he's gonna kill me over something," Otis said.

"Does-does-does he-he-he," Sammy blinked furiously like he was in pain. "Scuh-scuh-scare you-you?"

"Yes," Otis said.

"What do you say to him?" Leighton asked.

"I hold a pillow over my head. I don't think I've talked to him ever except when I scream for him to leave me alone," he said.

"Are there others?" Dr. Phillips asked.

"Molly is a bird I see," he said.

"What does she look like?" Dr. Phillips asked.

"She is bright blue and smiles like a cartoon. Most of the time she is perched near me and just smiles. I don't mind her," Otis said.

"Does she show up when the man is there?" Dr. Phillips asked.

"No, he scares her away," Otis said. "It's the same thing as Leighton in a different way. I know they're not real, but I can't believe it."

His voice was serious and defeated. It sounded like he couldn't continue fighting this, no matter how long he managed to keep his pulse. He folded his arms and leaned back in his seat. I was glad he kept looking at his lace-less boots. He didn't make eye contact with me and didn't acknowledge anyone unless they were speaking about him or to him. It might have been out of nervousness, but I wondered if he didn't want to see the man in his hallucinations staring at him, wondering why he was telling a bunch of strangers who could never see him just how scary a fictional person he was.

"Does the medication help?" Leighton asked.

"I can't really tell," Otis said.

"It takes time. That's just your body getting used to the medication you're taking, but please trust me when I say that time is the greatest factor in helping everyone here," Dr. Phillips said.

She turned to the man sitting in the chair a few seats away from everyone, directly facing Dr. Phillips. He was sitting with his body crunched together like a folding chair. His chin rested upon his hands as he leaned his elbows against his thighs. He covered his face with his palms and his fingertips locked his eyelids shut. His forearms were coated with tattoos. A snake wrapped around his right arm tightly with the head reaching the knuckles of his fingers. His left arm was coated with cursive letters making out the word 'Faithless' positioned perfectly between his elbow and wrist. He sat in silence though his breathing and occasional movement made it clear he was not sleeping.

"Isaac?" she asked, "Would you like to talk about anything?"

He mumbled in return, to which Dr. Phillips leaned forward in her chair.

"Sorry, I can't hear you, Isaac," she said.

He barely moved.

"Leave me alone," he mumbled louder.

Dr. Phillips returned to writing something in her clipboard and then smiled at me.

"Drew, would you like to talk about anything?" she asked.

I didn't want to look at Dr. Phillips. I just wanted to hear the calming sounds that filled my room back home. A few birds chirping nearby or my record player playing Howlin' Wolf's London Sessions while I looked up at the ceiling and time would finally stop, as if nothing mattered at all. But this was not my room back home.

No matter how those other patients could reveal themselves to strangers, I wondered if that too was something learned, like the first day at a new school and wondering if you'll ever learn where all your classrooms are. But then I began to wonder again if this was another ability that was not learned, but strictly based on capability. I wasn't capable of speaking to strangers and telling them my story though the bandages on my wrist already gave them a decent idea of why I was in the psychiatric wing.

I mumbled slightly, hoping it would beckon a non-participatory response, but I could sense everyone was still pre-occupied by my incomprehensible language. I decided to look at Dr. Phillips solely and simply shook my head. She smiled in understanding though her disappointment was slightly noticeable.

I glanced over at Isaac whose hands were woven through his hair that was oddly propped to one side of his face, so it covered one eye. It looked like he didn't have a chance of leaving this place just based on his desire to remain silent and I worried that I would one day become him.

"Am I ever going to leave this place?" I asked myself silently.

Chapter 10

Group ended after two hours. Everyone returned to the common room. I didn't know what to do except sit on the couch and wait for someone to turn on the television. Free time prevailed in this place, but boredom managed to overtake me. Little tasks such as getting my cigarettes from my room or using the bathroom only took up a few minutes of my time.

I wanted to be left alone without responsibility, but the constant checkups and outbreaks of patients who would scream out of the blue for reasons unknown were already bothering me like nails purposely running down a chalkboard.

Natalie circled around the room before leaning against the back of the couch.

"How are you doing, Drew?" she asked me.

I turned my body to see her chin resting on the couch's headrest.

"I'm fine," I said.

"Okay, just checking in," she said.

She patted me on the shoulder before walking away.

"How was group?" I heard Harlan's voice ask.

He walked around the couch and sat down right next to me.

"It was fine, I guess," I said.

"You talk?" he asked as he fell back into the cushion.

"No, I didn't know what to say," I said.

"Yeah, that starts to come naturally," Harlan said.

"Does it?" I asked.

"Yeah. You get used to hearing everyone else talk about why they're here. It gets easier to talk about yourself after a while," he said.

"That's good to hear. How was your group?" I asked.

"Fine," he said. "We just talk about our progress and stuff."

"How's that going for you?" I asked.

Harlan looked at me and shrugged, "Same old."

Harlan then turned away from me. He looked shell-shocked and tired. The dramatic headshaking with closed eyes coupled with a sigh told me something was off.

"Is it getting better, at least?" I asked.

"Can't tell," he said, "I can't tell."

I didn't know what I was supposed to say after this. Harlan held his head up by cupping his hands around his chin so his nails looked like they were gently trying to peel the skin off of his cheeks. I turned away from him and tried to focus on the television screen.

"Sorry," Harlan said suddenly.

I turned my attention back to him so my eyes were fixated on his thousand-yard stare.

"I didn't mean to put that shit on you," he said.

"It's fine," I said.

This seemed like the moment when I should grab his shoulder or pat his back, but an invisible presence stopped me before I could move my arms. Harlan maintained a wall between himself and the rest of the world, using nothing other than his silence and the mystery of what he could be thinking about. To the onlooker, one might say it was self-imposed, but when I looked at him sealing himself off from the rest of the psychiatric ward, whether it be by locking himself in his room, or simply just acting the way he did, I would say he was imprisoned by something.

"I'm sorry," he said before standing up.

"Harlan," I said, but he didn't acknowledge me.

He slowly walked around the couch and back to his room, arms lightly swaying against his hips with his eyes staring down at the tiles. He closed the door gently behind him while I continued to stare. I wanted to get help as I could only see him hanging from the ceiling in my head, but something told me that I should remain still. Psychiatric wards paint a strange picture for those who are not familiar. Solitude signals sickness, but something, a silent entity or maybe just your own morality tells you that that person needs to be alone. It's a strange contradiction between why it is some of us are here and what is sometimes needed to help us get out.

I stood up after a few seconds and pondered if a cigarette was the right call. Inexplicably, I just started walking to the side door that led to the outside stairwell. As I walked, I felt someone staring at me, waiting to see if I was walking to the door. I turned around and saw Lucky standing with a mop in his hands.

We stared at each other for a few seconds before I hesitantly nodded.

"I'm heading out," I said.

Lucky didn't say anything as he leaned the mop on the wall next to the yellow bucket. I started walking without him, but he caught up quickly through a few quick steps. He got in front of me and opened the door.

"Thanks," I said, letting the gust of wind blow my hair from my eyes.

I pulled out my pack of cigarettes from my pocket. It felt strange only having them in my pocket and I thought I was missing my belongings for a few seconds before remembering.

"What? Thought you lost something?" Lucky asked.

"Yeah, I forgot everything was taken," I said with a self-deprecating smile.

"Wait till you get in a car," he said as he handed me a lighter.

"Why?" I asked.

"Motion sickness," he said. "You won't realize it until you start moving, but it takes a little bit to get used to if you stay here awhile."

"Am I gonna stay here awhile?" I asked, taking the lighter and lighting my cigarette before giving it back to him.

"Honestly, Drew, I don't know. I don't mean this to sound like you should be here long, but suicide watch is a different ballpark. We can't accurately say that you're fine after a week, but that doesn't necessarily mean we have to keep you here for six months," he said.

I took a long drag from my cigarette, ashing it with a single flick of my finger. The wind took the fried remnants and sprinkled it through the small holes in the fence.

"Can I ask you something?" I asked Lucky.

"Shoot," Lucky said, folding his arms while he spat through the fence.

"What's wrong with Harlan?" I asked.

Lucky seemed to mull over his answer, as if he was running it over in his head on a loop, or deciphering if it was something he wanted to tell me.

"Harlan will need to tell you that," he said. "I don't want to be rude, but it's not my business to tell you what's going on with his life. I don't think that'll be fair if you find out through anybody but him."

He sighed and lightly kicked his foot against the ground.

"Did he do something?" Lucky asked.

"No, not to me. He just walked up and seemed down all of a sudden," I said.

"If you're thinking you did something, you didn't. He goes through bad spells sometimes. It makes it hard for him," Lucky said. "He'll be okay though."

We walked back inside once I was finished smoking. Lucky let me pass him and smiled at me gently as if to remind me that I was going to be okay. I returned to the common room and the dull television with static frames.

"Don't sit," Lucky said behind me.

"Why?" I asked him.

"They're going to call rec time in a few seconds," he said.

Just when he finished his sentence, I saw Natalie standing at the counter behind the glass. She pulled the microphone on the desk closer to her mouth.

"Recreation time, line up against the wall if you are going to head outside," she said. Her voice poured through the speakers in the ceiling.

A few people stood up from their seats. Others appeared from their rooms. I turned back to Lucky who was still standing behind me with his arms folded. His eyes followed me, but his body remained still.

"Is rec time mandatory?" I asked.

"No," he said, "it's just nice to get out of the building. It kills the smell of this place."

I followed Lucky's advice. Something in my head told me that behind the gray beard and singed eyebrows, a thirty-year experience knew better. We lined up against the wall, though it was only eight of us.

Natalie came out with a red-haired nurse who'd assisted in Jared's restraint before. They both stood next to Lucky as we followed one another out of the building and down the enclosed staircase I'd just been standing in.

As I emerged from the mask of shade lying on the ground by the door, I could smell the cigarette I recently had. I looked down as I planted my feet on each step towards the ground below. Dust particles had filtered down from the breeze and aligned within the cracks and crevices of chipped paint and poor masonry. We reached a turn where the stairwell ended and the path turned left from the metal fence enclosing the stairs. I followed the others in front of me and listened to the loose cement crunch under the stress of our shoes. The path was a blacktop walkway to the recreation yard.

I heard someone start whistling and I looked up to see a skinny frame clothed by a black hoodie standing in front of me. The figure walked a few steps further, but he turned slowly. I guessed he sensed my eyes on his back, silently characterizing him through the few traits that were visible to me. He glanced for only a few short seconds, seemingly just to figure out who was standing behind him. His hood came down over his eyebrows and the tilt of his head made it hard to get a picture of his face, but the green teeth and dreadlocks told me it was Otis.

I tried to scurry past him when the pathway ended and we were allowed to enter the concrete jungle that acted as the recreation center where there was a full-length basketball court and two handball courts on separate sides of a tall, white wall. Painted on the side facing me was a view of an ocean, from the sandy shores to the horizon where the blue sea disappeared under white clouds. Non-distinct as it might have been, it did have a certain degree of purpose in this place. Names were scrolled in black paint on the clouds.

I walked past Lucky, who was leaning against the brick wall of the building which cornered us in along with barbed wire fences on the other three sides.

"You like it?" he asked me.

"I guess so. I'm not one to really judge art," I said.

"A patient painted it a few years back," he said.

"Why are there names in the clouds?" I asked.

"People sign it if they want to when they leave," he said.

I nodded at him though I was wondering why they signed the clouds. It made it seem like the names were written in memoriam for those who left this place by way of their own hand. I wanted to ask Lucky about this, but I stopped myself. I'd learned a few things during the initial hours I'd spent in the psychiatric wing. Looney Tunes was the most ironic show to watch for those in the loony bin. Olga shouldn't ever be around the emotionally unstable, in any capacity whatsoever. A job existed where people would get paid to watch at-risk adults shower. Signatures in the clouds of those who'd been discharged was not something that I should have found strange.

I walked onto the basketball court and stood under the hoop. Someone was dribbling at the top of the key. I recognized Morgan immediately. I'd remembered his face when Jared urged him to continue his habit of smoking for a few pieces of gum. A few strands of black hair sprouted under his chin. His hair was jet black and cropped, closely knit to his cranium. He wore carpenter's jeans, spattered with paint and holes that looked like they'd been sheared as he ran through a hallway full of nails. His pants were tucked into two pairs of socks that came up to his calves and his Velcro sandals hugged his feet tightly, almost seeming to suffocate his ankles.

He shot a basketball towards the hoop. He laughed as he did so, chucking the ball from his hip with awkwardly positioned hands and body thrusts that looked like he was jumping into a pool. His feet flailed behind him, kicking the air to create enough thrust for the ball to reach the hoop. The ball fell short though, barely grazing the chain net and bounced high in the air before landing in my hands. I quickly threw a light bounce pass back to Morgan who fumbled it and nearly tripped over his own feet.

"Thank you," he said.

I nodded and continued walking to the far hoop. A lone basketball sat on the free throw line, perfectly centered, with the Jet logo facing me. The brown skin had worn, but it gave the ball character. I hated fresh balls from the bag. I loved the ones that looked like myself if I was an inflated piece of sporting equipment. I picked it up. The vibrations from dribbling hurt slightly, but I didn't want to stop playing. I hadn't touched a ball in months and this seemed like the perfect place to re-activate former pastimes. It beat all of my other choices.

The first shots felt terrible. My shoulders jittered every time I raised the ball to the right of my head. The ball lightly bounced out of my grasp as I went through the legs and behind the back.

A strange voice in my head came through and told me, *Oh shit. Oh shit.*

I remembered my mom telling me a story about her dad who'd been a high school star in the early 50s. They were once playing basketball in their backyard when she was in elementary school.

I remembered my mom talking about my grandpa's face when he dribbled off his foot on the way to the hoop. The ball clipped the toe of his shoe and went into the neighbor's yard. My mom told me he looked like he had aged more in that split second than he had in the past ten years. His hair looked grayer and he seemed to lose his once proud athletic splendor. The cheap smirk on his face followed by the dismal look he gave each of his palms told him a part of his life was over and there was no chance he could ever fully get it back.

I couldn't see myself in the same situation though. It wasn't the dirt outlining my fingerprints that I stared at; but instead, it was the bandages wrapped around my wrist and slight discoloration in my palms. I knew then that I was never going to be the same. My basketball skills suffered from lack of practice and that was something that could be managed. My mind, however, was scarred and it was public knowledge. Everything anybody wanted to know about my past would be answered through two ugly scars.

After ten minutes, my distances started to come back. Three-pointers no longer clanged off of the back of the rim or against the backboard. I started hearing that sweet sound of rubber pouring through the chain net. My hands started to hurt less as my mind drifted from my reality to the shot I was taking. I let the ball fall through my legs, guiding it with my fingertips as it wrapped around my back and one quick stutter step later left me finger rolling the ball through the basket without the help of the backboard.

It felt good. It reminded me of when I was in high school. Lacking ambition, responsibilities, and needing an escape from my home life, I would sit in the school gym for hours running off imaginary screens and letting the ball sail from NBA three-point range. I never thought about the death of my mother or my dad's bullshit or my siblings whom I could never compete with. I was simply living in the moment, shot by shot quite literally, and the feelings of despair and emptiness took a backseat to my amusement in hearing the metal chain rattle with each bucket.

I dribbled the ball out to the top of the key before sitting on top of it. I was breathing heavily and started rubbing my fingers, itching for a cigarette. My hands were dirty and only then did I realize that they were starting to get sore. My bandages were wrinkled badly and stained with soot from the ball. I cupped my hands over my eyes and listened to the wind rattle the nets on each side of the court.

The sound was interrupted, though, by a faint noise of shoes hitting the court. I turned to see Otis walking towards me. He waved at half court where his eyes met mine and silently asked if he could play with me. I stood up with the ball resting in between my bandaged arm and my hip.

"What's going on?" Otis asked.

"Hello," I said back.

"I'm Otis. We had group before this," he said.

"Right. Nice to meet you," I said.

I stuck my hand out and he met it with his. His grasp was firm, shockingly so being that his frame was so fragile. His teeth smiled at me displaying the green matte color that was similar to one on my index and middle finger from smoking.

"You mind if I shoot with you?" he asked.

"Yeah, sure," I lied.

I wanted him to disappear. It had nothing to do with him nor with my judgment. I tried not to do the latter. It didn't seem fair to him, being that I was there too. The only difference between us was our internal problems that stimulated nurses and shrinks with notepads and access to medical drugs that could cure us, but I still felt a burning desire to be alone.

Otis seemed friendly, but that didn't matter to me. He was a person with a brain who reached conclusions regarding those he met. I was soon to be a new conclusion as I'd never met him beforehand, nor was he related to me which would've forced a certain bond. A wave of heat funneled through my bloodstream and the tingling in my fingers appeared when I bounced the ball to Otis. Hot sweats overtook the former beads of cool sweat that slowly ran down my brow ridge.

I took a breath and turned away from him. I heard him start dribbling and glanced back. His meek figure effortlessly glided the ball through his legs. His fingertips took the ball down to his ankles before sending it through his legs, typing a figure eight. His dreadlocks swayed from under his hood as his body slightly shifted to let the ball pass through his legs undeterred. He quickly snatched the ball when he realized I'd been watching for a little.

"My bad. I just haven't touched a ball in a minute," he said.

"Really?" I asked. "It doesn't seem like it."

"I guess some stuff comes back quicker than others," he said.

Otis took one dribble and stepped into his shot near the top of the key. His form was nice. The ball left his right hand while his left fell off once he reached the apex of his jump. The ball glided off of his fingertips, fluidly spinning so the JET label was still easy to read. It clanged off of the back of the rim and shot back out to him. Otis groaned quickly while he reached for the ball and took another dribble. I remained standing at the free throw line and watched him put up another shot. His legs lifted his body from the black cement and he effortlessly released the ball again. I watched the slow spin connect with the net, dropping through without touching an inch of iron. The net jiggled and shot up through the hole it created. Similar to a pitcher whose throws make a popping sound against a catcher's mitt, a good shooter's ball swishes so that the net looks like it has imploded before reverting back to its old form.

"Thought you said you hadn't played in a while?" I asked.

"Yeah, some stuff just comes right back," he smiled.

I threw the ball back to him.

"Where are you from?" he asked.

"Hayley's Cove," I said.

"Goldencrest or Hayley's Cove?" he asked.

The question threw me off for a second. I had told people in the past I was from Haley's Cove and none of them ever questioned me.

"Goldencrest," I said hesitantly.

"Nice neighborhood," Otis smiled at me. "Why'd you say it like that?"

He took a few dribbles while he waited for me to answer.

"Sounds snobbish, I guess," I said.

"You're not a fan, huh?" He asked.

I shook my head.

"I know what you mean," Otis's said.

"Where are you from?" I asked.

"Upper East Side. Talk about snobbish. Those people are fucking parasites," he said.

He shot the ball and it ricocheted off the rim, popping straight up in the air before falling into my hands. Otis walked down to the block while I walked to the three-point line on the wing.

"Not a fan, I assume?" I asked him.

"Not one bit," he said curtly.

It was obvious he didn't want to talk about why he disliked it and I didn't blame him, but following this came the uncomfortable silence that one of us would eventually have to break.

"Did you play ball in high school?" I asked.

"Yeah, all four years," he said.

"Where did you go?" I asked.

"Chelsea Prep," he said.

"Really?" I asked excitedly.

"Yeah, why?" he asked me.

"I played for St. Thomas," I said. "We used to play you guys twice a year."

"No shit, I remember you clowns," Otis said and chuckled. "You guys had a weak ass crowd."

"I only played for the JV team, but your crowd still scared the shit outta me," I said. "They used to throw toilet paper at us when we walked out of the locker room for warm-ups."

"Yeah, we called them the gallery. I don't know why, but the name stuck," he said.

"When'd you graduate?" I asked.

"2010. You?" he asked.

"2015," I said.

Silence followed as I tried to figure out what had to happen for me to be standing in the same place as Otis.

"Wow," he said suddenly. "I never thought I'd run into anybody here that played for our arch rivals."

"Me neither," I said.

"Small world," Otis smiled.

"Yeah, small world," I said.

We shot around for thirty more minutes. My anxiety decreased during this time, but I still found myself calculating every word I'd said, putting space between him and myself. Otis wasn't like Harlan. Our conversation wasn't as natural. Whenever I met people like this, I needed my distance and my biggest fear was how they perceived me.

Lucky finally blew a whistle, signaling all of us to come back inside. I walked back up the stairs in a fog, my body unconsciously stepping correctly up the winding staircase. It was only when we walked into the ward that the warm air hit me and I found myself in a physically different place then I had been only seconds before. I walked past the orderlies and nurses on the way back to my room. Nerves kicked in and a rush of heat ran through me, vibrating my fingers and toes, as I tried to understand every word's impact on Otis.

I reached my room quickly and shut the door. Sleepiness revealed itself as my anxiety bordered on chaotic. Though I could comprehend the absurdity of what I was feeling, it didn't change how I felt. My worries only made me tired. The bed pulled me like a magnet and my legs collapsed once I reached the mattress. I didn't bother throwing the covers over my body, but simply rested with my limbs extended, stretching out my back before closing my eyes.

Chapter 11

I walked through the second floor of my former home, holding a flashlight. My steps were slow and uneasy as I made my way down the hall.

It was late at night though I didn't know what time. The digital clock next to my bed was blank since the wind knocked out a power line. The house was eerily quiet, though it should have been since it was early in the morning based on the darkness clouding the outside.

I walked slowly, pointing the flashlight at the mahogany floor and saw the white-painted wood holding up the banister. The light in my hand poked through the crevices between each slat of wood, lighting up family photographs on the walls that lined the staircase heading downstairs. I reached the balcony and grabbed the banister. I pulled myself to the end where the banister took a sharp turn to the right and acted as the second-hand railing leading down the stairs. I pointed the flashlight down the hall and saw the door to my parents' room.

I was scared of something popping out from one of the doors in the hallway. I wanted to run. I couldn't open my eyes for longer than a few seconds. The wood floor would creak under my small, bare feet and it would force me to shut my eyes tightly, so only the spatters of light that looked like an Alaskan night sky would appear. I felt like someone's hands were hovering over my shoulders, waiting for the perfect moment to pull me back while the flashlight fell to the floor, illuminating the force that was yanking my leg into a door down the hall. I took a few deep breaths and opened one eye at a time. Darkness still surrounded me, but the sound of rain and wind against the siding of the house made me hope someone else would wake up.

I finally reached my parents' room and banged on the door. "Mom! Dad!" I yelled.

The darkness felt like it was swallowing me as if I was a coal miner disappearing down a tunnel in a small railcar. The feeling in my stomach grew like a sandstorm, roiling my insides from my hips up to my sternum. The rain hit the windows with vigor and branches snapped as the wind grew too fierce. My hand slammed harder against the door. The gold doorknob rattled and chimed against its hinges, but it never rotated. Something crept closer to my neck. I thought I would feel fangs tearing at my skin or a claw pulling at my shirt.

I felt my weight crash as the door I'd been leaning on opened. I fell onto someone's feet and looked up to see my father's face. His belly hung over his pajama pants, but I could see his dark brown eyes glaring at me through the lightning strikes.

"Why don't you just fucking leave?" he yelled.

The windows shattered from the wind, but he didn't move as the rain started to pour onto the floor. He remained standing over me as I was pushed back by the force of the storm. I collected myself from the floor and used my hands to get back to a standing position. My father's hands reached out and tackled me. My skull crashed against the wood floor and my dad's weight crushed my chest. His hands wrapped themselves around my neck tightly, causing me to gasp for air while I flailed spastically, smacking my heels against the floor. I tried to move, but I couldn't lift my father's large frame. His eyes were exploding from his face as he started to scream.

"I told you once already. Never come back," he screamed.

My head was first to rise from my slumber followed by a long, dramatic breath. I grabbed my throat, feeling to see if there were any flesh wounds. I thought I felt the imprints of my father's stubby fingers, but when I felt the skin, nothing was there. Instead, I found my fingertips covered in sweat along with my palms. With every muscle that moved while I went to stand up, I noticed my entire body was covered in sweat. My skin stuck to my shirt and jeans. I let my feet hit the floor while I rested on the edge of the bed. The smell of myself nearly made me gag. I felt putrid and oddly sticky, like someone covered me in post-it glue. I stepped off the bed and onto the floor.

I could only think of Otis for some reason. I hated living in the same building as people I couldn't get away from. In the past,

I was great at making excuses or saying 'no' when I felt I would be better off alone, but here my main excuse was I have to use the bathroom, and I couldn't even do that by myself.

I grabbed the tub of soap and the bottle of shampoo along with a fresh pair of boxers and a T-shirt. I didn't care if I needed to use my old clothes as a towel. The simple solitude and normalcy of having a shower without being observed was reason enough. I started to walk through the door, overjoyed by the lack of an authority figure nearby, but was interrupted when I found Natalie standing outside.

"Hey, Drew, just need to check…" her face seemed surprised as she looked at what I was holding, "in," she finished.

She folded her arms and chuckled to herself.

"Were you gonna use your shirt?" she asked.

"No," I said.

"I know this sucks, Drew, but I have to accompany you to the bathroom," she said.

"I know. I wasn't gonna go alone," I said.

She looked at me, through the lies and self-loathing.

"Drew, you know the rules. Follow them or else we're going to be doing this for a lot longer than you'd like," she said.

"I know. I'm sorry," I said.

I hung my head in shame. I never liked lying despite my poorest attempts at convincing myself that I never did. Natalie grabbed the plastic sleeves I needed to wear and a towel from the nurses' station and then followed me to the bathroom. I heard a shower nozzle already protruding water from its pores. The steam had built up in the room and the mirror was layered in fog.

"Ah, ha, ha, ha, stayin' alive. Well, now, I…" a voice shrilled before mumbling the remaining chorus.

I recognized it quickly. It was Morgan's voice lacking the nerves and hesitancy I heard when Jared tricked him into giving away his gum. I walked into the stall a few doors away from Morgan's. I hung my dirty clothes on the hanger and the fresh ones on the other hanger, mirroring what I had done the day before. Natalie grabbed the towel from me and hung it on the hanger set up on the stall door. I turned back around to Natalie once I was in my boxers. She held two plastic sleeves in her hands and helped me put them on.

"You still have to watch me?" I asked.

Natalie looked at me, her eyes replete with empathy. I knew I was clawing at her conscience. She blew one sympathetic gasp and let her head sag in the humid moisture encompassing the room.

"Yes," she said.

My fear returned, paralyzing me until I shook uncontrollably as I reached for the shower dial. I could sense Natalie wishing she didn't have to stand a few feet from me, but the reality was that she did and it wasn't going to change for a little while. She stood away from the sliding door, but her presence locked it in its ajar position.

I took off my boxers and showered quickly. This place robbed you of the simplest indulgences. A peaceful shower, a morning cigarette, a few evening cigarettes, and good crap all came with a price tag.

After I pulled on my fresh clothes, minus the jeans I was re-wearing, Natalie took me to the sink to check my bandages again. I watched in the mirror while her calm, motherly face, devoid of beauty and covered with middle-aged freckles stared at my wrists. The bandages lost some of their stickiness, but were still covering my wired wounds.

"These we can leave until tomorrow morning," Natalie said.

Natalie followed behind me again as I went back to my room. She poked her head around the door as I kicked my worn clothes into the corner, making a small pile.

"I'll be back in 15 to check on you," she said as I handed her my towel.

"I'll be around," I said.

Natalie smiled and left. I sat on my bed and waited for something to happen. Time passed like corrosion. I dangled my legs and cracked my knuckles, waiting for the seemingly inevitable sound of footsteps creeping down the hall or screaming at the top of someone's lungs. It felt like an hour passed with the hallway only emitting small chatter and television cartoons, but I only realized I'd sat in the same position for a quarter of an hour when Natalie walked back in.

"Hey, just checkin' in. At 12:30, we're having lunch," she said.

"What time is it now?" I asked.

"12:15," she said.

I nodded at her as she wrote something on her clipboard. I looked down at my feet again and let my body slide out of the bed before putting on my moccasins.

I walked out of the room and into the hallway. I could see the top portion of black cartoon outlines combined with the audible sounds of 1950s animation. I walked closer to the group, wondering where I was going to sit.

An old man sat at the window. The sun caught his wrinkled skin so it looked like it was peeling off of him like plastic wrap. His glasses were large, the size of Aviators with prescription lenses. His Adam's apple swam up and down his throat with every painful breath he drew. Drool seeped from his lips, clinging to his chin before plummeting onto his lap.

I looked over at the faces on the couch. I noticed Sammy sitting with his legs folded like a pretzel. He smelled bad though no one nearby seemed bothered by it. The man I noticed yesterday with a pack of cigarettes tucked into the folded fabric of his beanie sat with his eyes partially covered. His black shorts and lace-less sneakers were propped up on the ottoman in front of him. His face was long and blank, lacking any expression. I felt sorry for him. He fidgeted for a second and I was worried he was going to notice me, so I went to an empty chair by the window.

I sat down, put my feet up against the window ledge and stared off into the grass just beyond the tall fence surrounding the recreation yard. I imagined the smell of fresh air when I knew I wouldn't have to walk back into a hospital. I thought of the beach near my house where I would sit and smoke as the waves crashed onto the sand near my feet. I started to smell everything again and I closed my eyes. The ocean made me philosophical for no reason other than the strangeness of watching the water swirl like a Twizzler.

The night would come and boat lights would flicker in the distance like fireflies while the water rush remained constant. My shirt would brush against my skin gently with every breeze while birds flew overhead. The light of my cigarette would burn sweet as the smoke pooled in my lungs. Burned filters would sit between my extended legs in a pile of other partially fried cigarettes and I'd light up another when my inner addict would say so a few minutes later. I could sit and stare as the night would fall over me and then I could simply bask in my own self-pity when my eyelids felt heavy. When I would stand to leave, I would realize that I would be back tomorrow, away from all the bullshit before the bullshit comes and finds me.

"Drew," Natalie said from behind me. "You okay?"

"Yeah," I said and rubbed my eyes.

"Okay, well, we're all heading down to eat," she said.

I followed as Natalie led me down the stairs to the cafeteria. We walked in with the other patients and I joined the line to be served. I watched as the two gothic girls sat at a table, each with a full tray of food. A brunette, middle-aged nurse sat across from them. One of the girls flicked her peas and carrots while the other stuck her plastic fork into her slice of pizza. The woman leaned over the table and started talking to the girls, ushering them towards the food when one of the girls unexpectedly lifted her tray and slammed it on the floor. The cafeteria fell silent as the nurse called for Dougie.

"I'm not fucking eating," the girl screamed.

Dougie ran over from the corner nearest the entrance door. He gently wrapped his arms around her and guided her to the stairs. The brunette nurse walked over to the door and opened it for them. They disappeared into the stairwell, but her screams echoed in the distance like the haunting sound I imagined hearing if I watched someone being pulled into oblivion.

I walked up to the counter where a woman handed me a plate just like the one the girl refused to eat. A slice of greasy pizza, a small pile of peas, and four fat carrots with a carton of lemonade. Walking back into the cafeteria, I searched again for a lonely place to sit and found the seat I was in just a few hours before. Natalie sat at the far end of the table and read something from a beige folder, periodically looking over at me and the rest of the room. I ate silently and stared down at my wrists. I then felt the table shutter and looked up to see Leighton putting her tray down across from me.

"Drew, right?" she said.

"Yeah, Leighton?" I asked.

She nodded her head and I stuck my hand over the table. She saw my bandaged wrist and though I wondered if she noticed them before during group therapy, then I knew for certain that she had more knowledge about me than I was willing to give up.

"Nice to meet you," I said.

"You too," she responded.

"Do you mind if I sit here?" she asked.

"No, not at all," I said.

"Thanks," she said and sat down on the stool.

I returned to my plate and silence ensued for a few seconds as she opened her paper carton of lemonade and took a sip.

"You're new here, right?" she asked.

"Yeah. That obvious, huh?" I asked.

"Kind of. I haven't seen you around ever, so I took a wild guess that you might be new," she said.

A grin formed across her face and it eased my nerves. I smiled back and let out a quiet laugh.

"Where are you from?" she asked.

"Hayley's Cove," I said.

"Where's that?" she asked.

"About forty minutes from the Hamptons," I said to which she nodded. "What about you?"

"Manhattan. I'm from the Bowery," she said.

"Oh, wow, I went to high school down there," I said.

"No kidding. Where?" she asked.

"St. Thomas," I said.

"Really? I live a few blocks from there. I went to St. Mary's around the corner. I probably saw you before," she said.

"Wow. Small world," I said.

"For such a big city," she said.

Her teeth were fluorescent white and her T-shirt hugged her body. She'd changed into tight jeans that grasped tightly around her ankles while her feet clung to a pair of brown flip-flops.

"How long have you been in, if you don't mind me asking?" I asked.

"A week and a half. How do you find it here?" she asked.

"I don't really know. I haven't been here long enough," I said and shrugged my shoulders.

"It gets easier," she said.

"I hope," I said. I was lost for words. I was enamored by her calmness. Her voice was raspy, but heavenly sweet. I wanted to ask what she was doing here and though I'd heard some of her life's story beforehand, I wanted to know more. How could she have ended up here?

"Trust me. My first few days were rough, but you start to get acclimated," she said.

I nodded, but I didn't truly believe her.

"Yeah, I just have a hard time believing I'm here, you know? It's just hard to come to grips with," I said.

I didn't know why I said that. It seemed appropriate at the time, but I felt my walls of solitude cracking like a dam with spurts of water running through. Leighton's voice soothed me and I felt like I could talk to her despite just meeting her.

"I know what you mean. Sometimes I look around and wonder how I got here too," she said.

Silence again ensued for a few moments while we ate.

"I'm sorry if this offends you and it's fine if you don't want to answer, but how do your wrists feel?" she asked me.

"Oh, that's not offensive. They're okay, I guess," I said nervously.

"They'll probably look better than this," she said and lifted her wrist parallel to her head. She turned her palm towards me. Long scars ran down her bronze arm. Her smooth skin made the scars seem like dried riverbeds. They shouldn't have been there, but internally, I was glad they were. I didn't feel alone in this place. I thought that maybe I wasn't as crazy as I thought I was.

We talked some more and Leighton finished her food quickly. She threw out the rest of her tray and walked to the exit door. She turned back to me and waved shyly. I smiled back and watched her disappear silently into the stairwell.

Similar to what happened with Otis, I found myself going over my conversation with Leighton line by line. My stomach churned and twisted. I felt my intestines starting to wrap tighter inside my body and lost my appetite entirely. I got angry and started cursing myself silently. I wished I was able to hear her thoughts and conclude accurately that none of them involved me. I didn't know what Leighton was thinking about and it made me worry that I had said something wrong or came off as someone I wasn't.

Why was I the one who had to think this way? I thought to myself.

I picked up my tray which was nearly as full as when I received it. I dumped it in the trash and looked around the room. Most of the people had left. I hadn't seen Otis or Harlan. I wanted to make sure Harlan was okay, but I guessed I missed him in the cafeteria. Natalie exited with me, guiding me back upstairs. I walked down the hallway and tried to think of something to do. My room was a hole with a bed and the common room was home to all of those whom I feared, those being people.

As I walked with Natalie, she tailed off and went into the nurses' station.

"I'll be back in fifteen minutes, Drew," she smiled.

"Okay," I said.

I continued down the hallway, glancing at the partially closed doors and tried to slow my pace in order to get a peek of who was inside them. I heard someone inside one of their rooms.

"Get away. Get away!" he yelled. "Leave me alone!"

The door flew open and Otis came running out. He swayed in the hallway while I backed away from him as he grabbed his temples in agony.

"Get outta my fuckin' head," he yelled.

His hood had fallen off his head and I got my first full sight of the dreadlocks he donned. His fingers were tangled within them, suddenly ripping two of them off as he tried to quell whatever was in his head. He fell to the ground as the nurses came running out of their booth. Dougie appeared at the other end of the hall after coming out of the bathroom. He ran towards us. Natalie grabbed me and led me away from Otis while a red-haired, skinny nurse and the nurse who had been watching the gothic girls eat ran over to him. The red-haired woman brought a wheelchair. The other nurse lifted Otis's sleeve and sterilized his arm.

"Don't move, Otis. This will make you feel better," she said and stuck the needle into his arm.

Otis didn't resist, but he grimaced like his head was going to implode and some creature would stumble out. As the injection sent whatever fluid it was into his bloodstream, his face became less stressed and his muscles relaxed so his teeth didn't crush each other. His head fell slowly until it leaned against the wall. Blood ran from his head where two of his dreadlocks used to be. Natalie came with towels thrown over her shoulder and put them over his wounds. Dougie lifted him by his armpits and propped Otis so he sat comfortably in the wheelchair. The nurses fixed his legs so his feet rested on the foot pedals.

"Bring him to observation. I'll call Dr. Phillips to let her know the situation," Natalie said.

Dougie didn't respond audibly; instead, he started walking back towards the elevator down the hall.

I walked past the nurses who picked up the severed threads of hair and used the spare towels Natalie brought to clean up the blood. Lucky appeared with a mop and a bucket of water. I didn't know what to do so I stood still and leaned against the wall, breathing slowly as I tried to comprehend what I'd just seen. Lucky saw me and dropped the mop, letting it land loudly on the floor. He came over and stood next to me.

"You okay, Drew?" he asked.

"Yeah," I said as I calmed myself. "Never seen anything like that before."

Lucky nodded his head in understanding and put his hand over my shoulder.

"Things happen here that you should never see. I'm sorry. I really am. But know that we are here to help. You'll be just fine," he said to me.

I nodded at him and took one long breath, sending my head to lean against the wall. Another breath and my heart rate slowed to its normal speed. The pulse in my neck no longer churned like a piston.

"You're okay. Go take a seat in the common room. It will calm you down," Lucky said as he let go of my shoulder.

He walked me to the couch and I was glad to see only a few people. A woman sat in a chair facing the window reading a book. Her hair covered the back of her chair and I could only see her shaky hands turn the page to a thin paperback book, the pages covered in coffee stains and hand-drawn stars. I saw the man with the beanie playing cards with an imaginary friend at a table for two.

"Don't be so silly, Billy, I know you don't have that hand," he said.

I sat on the couch and put my legs on the ottoman. I didn't like how others could be watching from behind me like I had done before lunch, but it was open space for the rest of us to share. Egos collided and my presence as a newly appointed ward victim didn't know what to expect, but based on my observations of people in the past, I had a feeling I would soon find out. That knowledge terrified me to the brink of running through the window and face planting onto the concrete below.

I found the remote sitting on the edge of the ottoman and used it to flick through the channels. I passed the cartoons and news programs before finding ESPN just as the theme song played through the speakers at the bottom of the television. I watched as the anchors reviewed Thursday Night Football between the Rams and the Saints.

I let my shoulders relax and stretched my legs that had grown sore from playing basketball a few hours earlier. I watched deep throws spiral perfectly under the dome lights and land right in the receiver's hands two yards short of the end zone. The receiver galloped across the goal line and spiked the ball as hard as he could into the AstroTurf.

Realization came next, however, the revelation that I was actually still here. I thought I'd noticed this in my first session with Dr. Phillips, but the stage had altered itself. This wasn't a dream. I was here in the thick of what I imagined this place to be. My presence forced a spotlight to shine overhead and I waited for the doctors to surround me with clipboards and notebooks, jotting down every single irregularity I'd displayed. It was then that I remember thinking again, 'Holy shit. I'm a psychiatric hospital patient'.

I felt someone behind me, the way a crow looks your way when you try to take a picture of it. I leaned my head back so my eyes saw the hallway upside down. A bald head greeted me with a chin covered in scruff. Jared stood with his arms folded. When my eyes met his, he walked around the couch and sat down next to me. He sniffled once and kept his arms folded while he let his legs extend fully. His heels bounced up and down against the tile floor. His eyes stared directly into mine, though I tried my best to look away, but I continued to feel his glare.

"What's up?" I asked.

His boots continued smacking against the floor and he cracked his fingers using his thumbs. They sounded off like firecrackers. I looked at every facet of his appearance. He rested his right arm on his leg, scratching his fingers around his denim-covered kneecap. His knuckles turned white as his nails scraped harder against his jeans. I looked up and found his eyes still gazing into mine. The menacing possibility that he would leap with his arms extended and strangle me or pound my face in with the heel of his combat boot both felt like realistic outcomes. I grabbed the remote and put it in the space between us on the couch before standing up and walking silently away.

When I started back towards my room, I heard him laugh. His laugh overwhelmed the hall, careening off of the walls like a handball. The feeling that I was being watched had disappeared and a new feeling crashed upon my shoulders, sending a heat strike down my spine. It was the undesired spotlight, the kind that comes with humiliation. I didn't turn around fully, but I twisted my head so my chin nearly leaned on my shoulder. I saw Jared's boots on the armrest which I had been using. His feet were crossed over one another. They fluctuated back and forth quickly, hitting against one another like Newton's cradle. Others turned to see Jared as he flicked through the channels while his body twisted and arched with every menacing laugh. I felt the others looking at me and I turned from them as soon as I became aware of their eyes. They didn't need to tell me their understanding. It was practically scrawled across the hollowed look they each gave me.

My frustration boiled over and I felt the nerves in my stomach anchoring themselves to my ribs. I wanted to scream, but instead, I went into my room while I listened to the echoes of Jared's laugh droning on. I walked into my room and looked out at the sky through the prison bars. I turned the light out and closed the door.

Reaching my bed, I pulled the covers over my head and sank my teeth into the fabric. My mouth salivated as I began to cry. The sheet turned soggy and tears fell from my eyes as I wished for this nightmare to end. I heard a knock on the door and rolled over.

"Drew," Natalie said as she opened the door.

I turned my body over and stared into the holes that were in the wall, pretending to be asleep.

"Okay," she said to herself and left.

I laid there for a while. I didn't know the schedule for the day's activities and I didn't really care. Natalie came in four times after that and hadn't said a word. I just heard her pen marking the clipboard which I assumed meant I was still alive.

The fifth time she came back though, she walked to the edge of my bed.

"Drew, we have activities in fifteen minutes," she said.

I didn't want to answer. I didn't even know how to do so. My body remained still, but the sniffling and saliva that cluttered my throat caught her attention.

"Are you okay?" she asked.

"I don't know," I said with a traumatized voice complete with slurs and sniffling.

"Hang in there. I'll be back with Dr. Phillips in a second," she said and closed the door.

I heard the footsteps jogging down the hall towards Dr. Phillips's office. My legs felt heavy and unusable while my arms sagged and I looked at my wrists. I pried off the bandages and looked at the swollen skin held together by stitches. I ran my fingers across the cuts that could potentially sever me from reality.

I stopped once I heard voices speaking to one another just outside my door, the subject of their conversation being me. Over their voices though, I heard one particular voice, a voice that would visit me every day following.

"I promise," I muttered, "I promise."

* * *

I woke to the early morning grayness the following day. I'd slept on and off the previous day, only leaving my room to take my medication when they called my name over the loudspeaker. An empty chair sat in the doorway and I wondered who'd been watching me through the night.

I rose and felt the sweat that had filtered into my jeans and I quickly took them off in search of fresher attire. Changing into a plain red shirt and gym shorts, I put on my moccasins and walked to my door, sidestepping the empty chair and stepping into the hallway.

"Drew," Dr. Phillips said quietly.

I turned and saw her walking out of the women's bathroom.

"Morning, Dr. Phillips," I said once she was within a few feet of me. "Did you watch me through the night?"

"No, I just took over for Natalie a few minutes ago so she could get some coffee. You're up early," she said.

"Yeah, slept a lot yesterday," I said.

"Well, the alarm doesn't ring for a little while. Could we have a word in my office?" she asked. "Or do you want to wait until after breakfast?"

"Now's fine," I said and knew she wanted to talk about the night before.

The doors to each room were closed and only the sound of a vent in the ceiling came from the hallway. I followed behind Dr. Phillips whose high-heeled boots struck the floor with that amazing sound.

We reached Dr. Phillips's door and she let me walk in first. I remained standing upon entry into her office until she was present within the room as well.

"Please, sit," she said.

I nodded and sat. She walked to the other side of her desk and sat gracefully in the leather computer chair. Dr. Phillips placed her hands on the arms of her chair and looked at me though I tried to avoid her stare by focusing on her wall of scholastic achievements or reading the book titles residing on her bookshelf.

"Can we talk about last night?" she asked.

"I guess I don't have a choice," I said.

"No, no, I guess not. I told you I talked with Dr. Merriweather, right?" she asked me.

"Yes," I nodded my head.

"He told me you have a history of excessive sleeping," she said.

"Yeah, it's been a bit of an issue," I said.

Dr. Phillips nodded her head.

"Drew, I need you to work with us. Please let us help you," she said.

"I know," I said.

I tilted my head and licked my lips. I tried to spew up the few words I'd been thinking of, but they'd cemented themselves in the back of my throat.

"Go ahead," Dr. Phillips said and leaned her head forward.

I took one long breath before I uttered the words that seemed like the only thing that would help me cling to life for the sake of those who I managed to hurt.

"I promise," I said.

Chapter 12

A week and a half had passed since I promised a second person I would try to survive.

I'd followed the consistent routine of being observed at all times. Waking up, taking a new medication I'd been prescribed called Nortriptyline, eating breakfast, going to group therapy, recreation time, then lunch, then come back for free time where I tried to either kill seconds in my room staring at the ceiling or reading one of the few books offered at the nurses' station. Then, I'd go to another therapy session with one of the nurses where we'd combat negative thoughts by writing five positive ones about ourselves. And then you tell others amazing things about them despite not really knowing any of them, then one of the nurses, either Natalie or Helen, the red-haired nurse, reiterated the hospital's support guidelines that reveal not taking your medication is harmful to you and the work the staff is trying to do.

After this, we ate dinner and came back upstairs where Dr. Phillips held up a selection of movies in which we, the patients, at least the functioning ones, voted on which they wanted. The movie choices ranged from *Stand by Me* to *Big Hero Six* to *The Notebook* to *Mamma Mia* to a bootleg copy of *Baby Boss*. I thought *Stand by Me* would offer a future plethora of interesting film selections, but I was mistaken, though it's not to say those movies weren't entertaining. They'd even given us popcorn sometimes.

After the movie ended, we'd be called up for our nightly round of medication and then we would be allowed to hang out in the common room or in our rooms until ten o'clock. Then they would call lights out and either Natalie, Olga, or Helen would sit in my doorway watching me sleep until the alarm sounded at 7:30 the following morning and the cycle would repeat itself.

Riley visited me five more times. Twice with Brock. Every conversation was less painful than the one before. Their visits gave me time to breathe and a pure moment in which I didn't feel so incarcerated.

I wasn't healthy enough yet to be left alone on the outside, but there was something about time that lessened some of my pain. I grew more comfortable around the others and my initial fear of their judgments had diminished some as I talked to them more often. I didn't hear my father's voice spewing through the letter he'd given me. I was able to somewhat block it out after a week or so, but it never went away entirely. I came to the conclusion that it never would.

The reasons I was here were embedded in my identity. Understanding as opposed to quivering with the reminder of my worst moments was a battle that penetrated every aspect of my life. The constant voice I spoke to myself with and only to myself was like a ghost that haunted me. It resided solely where no one could see it, but it was an aspect I would have to explain at some point to those who were close to me.

I didn't talk to Harlan once during this time. I'd seen the nurses outside his room while he slept with the covers over his head. He just remained in his bed for all hours of the day while I wondered what had caused his withdrawal. I wondered if I had said something or if I had made him uncomfortable, since my first day on the ward was when he shut down. I didn't see him in group therapy, instead, Dr. Phillips had him in her office for one-on-one meetings. I wanted to talk to him, but he seemed like he just wanted to be left alone.

Harlan finally returned to group therapy and we were put in the same section. Dr. Phillips had us sit in a circle, the same way we always did.

"So who wants to start today?" she asked.

We looked around the circle and waited for someone to either get called on or raise their hand hesitantly. I was slightly shocked when Harlan raised his. His corduroy pants and suede shoes looked the same as they had the first day I'd met him. I noticed his Rush T-shirt with sleeves that were too long for what I had normally seen him wear. It looked like he lost weight though he was already skinny when I first met him.

"Thank you, Harlan. Everyone give your eyes and ears," Dr. Phillips said.

Harlan smiled to himself and it became apparent from the seconds of silence that followed that he was nervous.

"Hello, everybody, um, I, um, I'm struggling with my Bipolar Disorder. I haven't been able to move really and I haven't eaten much either, but it's getting better every day. I find that the medication is helping, but it's still a struggle," he said.

His voice sputtered through most of the words. His body didn't look relieved when he finished. It seemed like this was something that would always weigh on him and I never got the feeling that he believed he could beat it. I wondered if that was why he wanted to speak because it didn't matter if he did or didn't.

"Has it gotten better over the past week?" Dr. Phillips asked.

"Yeah, I think so. It's just frustrating when it comes back and I have to deal with it," Harlan said.

I understood what he meant. Frustration is an understatement. When my symptoms would return, I would always wonder if they would leave, the same way I thought sunburn never would. Some days are better than others, but waking up in the morning without knowing how my stomach was going to feel or what thoughts would be in my head ate away at me.

"Anyone else want to chime in?" Dr. Phillips asked.

I thought for a second about doing so, but instead of contemplating the consequences, I decided to just go for it.

"Yes, thank you, Drew," she said when she saw my hand raised.

"Well, I know what you mean, Harlan. I've been struggling with depression and severe anxiety for a few years now. Some days I feel fine, but other days I wake up and I think that I've regressed again. That strange shift between feeling fine and sinking back into the past is really annoying to deal with after a while. It's not something that can be romanticized either. It's just a pain in the ass to deal with. Kind of plain and simple," I said.

It felt good to talk in the group. I had feared how others might think about me if I did speak, but I'd realized that I wasn't here by mistake. I was there just like everyone else. We had issues that none of us could hide from.

"Yeah," Harlan said, "It's not like everything goes away. Those feelings always come back at some point. It isn't like they disappear. It makes you wonder if you're getting better."

"Yes, you are," Dr. Phillips said. Her voice acquired a serious tone, "Please, everyone, do not let yourself believe that you can't get better. Bad episodes will come back occasionally. That's not unusual, but treatment will get you to the point where these are controllable. Granted, you will think about them, but you won't be greatly affected by them like you were in the past."

After we ended, Harlan came up to me.

"Drew," he said.

"What's up?" I asked. "How're you doing?"

"I wanted to say sorry about the past week. I'm not trying to avoid anybody or anything. I'm just fucked up sometimes and shit fucks with me," he said.

The anxiety released me from its grasp and I smiled, happy to know I was not the reason he was feeling the way he was. Rationally thinking, I didn't know what I could have done that would have made him behave the way he had, but that rationality didn't affect my emotions.

"It's fine. I wanted to make sure I didn't say anything that got you upset," I said.

"Nah, you didn't do anything. I just have these weird spurts where I get in a funk," he said.

"Well, good that you're feeling better now," I said.

"Yeah, I guess I do," he paused. "You wanna mess around with the guitar?"

"Yeah sure," I said.

I followed Harlan to his room after he asked Natalie if she could grab the guitar from the arts and crafts room. She did and we took turns messing around with it, but mostly talked with each another. We talked about anything other than why we were here. We covered everything from music to books to movies. I enjoyed being around Harlan again. Like the first time we'd hung out, it felt nice to forget where we were and what we suffered from. Instead, it was strictly bullshitting without the slightest care that we would have to explain this to others for the rest of our lives.

Natalie came in later and told us to go downstairs for lunch. Harlan and I continued talking when we went down to the cafeteria, even when Jared came forward to yell at us for not hanging out with him at his table. Our respective smiles and polite disagreement made us laugh once he stomped away.

Leighton joined us. We'd eaten together over the past week. She'd gotten tired of sitting with the gothic girls who constantly threw their food or threw it up the second they finished swallowing a single bite. They still sat in the back of the cafeteria, but they had started to get through their lunch without outlandishly reacting, though I would still see tears forming in their eyes while their forks shook uncontrollably from the tremors running through their hands.

After lunch, the three of us started walking upstairs to the common room. We hoped to get up there before the others so we could watch television at least for a few minutes. Natalie followed behind us since she still had to accompany me everywhere. I didn't like knowing she was always a few steps behind, but thankfully, she would hold herself back a few feet so her presence wasn't stifling.

Once we got upstairs, I was about to follow them to the couch when Natalie grabbed my shoulder.

"Dr. Phillips would like to see you now. Sorry, I forgot to tell you she wanted you in after lunch," she said.

"It's fine. Let's go," I said.

Natalie led me to Dr. Phillips's door, which she knocked on. Dr. Phillips opened it and politely ushered me in while Natalie smiled before walking back to the nurses' station. Her eyes met mine as I waited for her to tell me to be seated.

"Drew, you can just sit. You don't have to wait for me to tell you to do so," she said as she closed the door.

"Oh, sorry, just a habit, I guess," I said.

I sat in the chair and sank into the cushion. Dr. Phillips went to her desk and opened a drawer. She picked up a stack of papers held together by a rubber band. Her hands twirled the band around so it snapped onto her wrist. I let my eyes peer over the desktop accessories, the mug full of pens, the snow globe circling around a small scale Yankee Stadium, the bent neck of a tabletop lamp, and the beige folders with typed names glued to the top right corners of each.

She turned the papers vertically and banged them on the desktop so they lined up evenly before holding them up to me. I grabbed them from her gently and started to read. I saw the title page and recognized it immediately. Sprawled across the top of the masthead read 'The Last Eight Months'. I then read my name that was inked into the center of the page.

"I asked Dr. Merriweather to send me some of your stuff. He sent me this," she said.

I glanced at her momentarily before searching through the pages. I re-read the words that once sounded so good. Now I felt they were choppy and lacked any potential for a career in writing. I'd come to that conclusion years ago, but this was an unpleasant reminder of what I could never achieve.

"Did you read it?" I asked.

"Yes, I did," she said as she finally sat in her chair. "I must say it is good. I know I should have asked, but I was intrigued by it. Dr. Merriweather holds your abilities in high regard."

"Thanks," I said unenthusiastically.

"You don't sound convinced," she said.

"What is there to be convinced about?" I asked.

"The work. It really is good. From our job standpoint, Dr. Merriweather and I cannot lie to you. We're not allowed to. I'm not saying this to get you out of here. I'm saying it because it's the truth," she said.

"I understand. Dr. Merriweather told me the same thing. For whatever reason though, I still don't believe it," I said.

"Why not?" she asked.

"Don't know," I said. "It just doesn't feel real to me."

"When's the last time you wrote something? Anything? A journal entry? A story? A poem? A joke?" Dr. Phillips asked.

I thought back and saw my notebook, collecting dust on top of my dresser. Cobwebs were laced through the metallic silver spirals while a pen sat atop the notebook with the bookmark strap ripped into two strands. I thought about my drawer in the bureau near my nightstand lined with journals, loose pages covered in notes, and old short stories I never showed anybody.

I missed how the free-flowing movement of the pen sounded as it marked loose-leaf pages with a sharply curled 'g' and a bubble 'r'. It'd been a long time since I'd had that feeling. I knew I missed it, but it didn't miss me. The pages I held in my hands told me I would never be good enough to become a writer, but I wished they spoke just so I could prove it to everyone else.

"It's been awhile," I said.

"Awhile as in a month or six?" Dr. Phillips asked.

"Now? Probably seven," I said.

"Why'd you stop?" she asked.

"My dad never liked when I did it, but once I started to feel worse, I had a hard time getting back into it," I said.

"By 'started to feel worse', you mean dealing with depression?" she asked.

"Yes," I said.

"Are you feeling better now after getting used to the hospital and such?" she asked.

"Yes, I think so. I still have bad days like I said during group, but it's not as intense as it was before," I said.

Dr. Phillips sat quietly for a moment. Her eyes looked into mine. I tried to avoid them by looking away.

"Well," Dr. Phillips started, "I'm going to do two things. One is I'm taking you off suicide watch..." she said.

"Really?" I interrupted her.

My eyes widened and a strange expression crossed my face. It was one of joy and confusion. I didn't know how to react to the news. It was a strange phenomenon in a way. Similar to being honored as the greatest minor league baseball player or the world's richest poor person. It was an achievement of sorts, but a rather dubious one.

"Yes," she smiled. "I think you have adjusted nicely and I don't believe you're a threat to yourself or others. I believe your attempt at ending your life was a response to a really bad day, to put it shortly," she said.

"To put it lightly," I quipped.

"Yes, that too. And secondly, I am going to have you write something for me. This can be anything from a poem to a joke to a story to a novella. I do not care whether it is good or not. I just want to see something that you've written," she said.

I looked at her and swallowed the saliva that had built up in the back of my throat. My fingers danced against my leg and I could feel my toes tapping against the floor.

"How do you feel about that?" she asked.

"I think I think about being good at writing more than I truly am good at it. I think I find myself sleeping more when I try to write or think about ideas. I get tired and then fall asleep, no matter what time of day it is," I said.

"Do you love writing?" Dr. Phillips asked.

"Well, yeah, but I don't think others like my writing," I said.

"I'm not worried about that right now. Drew, you might not think this, but you are talented. Dr. Merriweather told me about his goals with you, the first being get you to write because it will help you," she said.

"It just makes me angry though," I said.

"Drew, I love my job and sure there are times it drives me nuts, but I love what I do. You strike me as someone who wants to do what they love. Am I right?" she asked.

I nodded my head.

"Okay, and if you love this, you need to chase after it. I cannot promise you anything in the future, but I can promise you this, if you don't try, you'll never have a chance," she said.

Her words were effective. They weren't sugar-coated, they were curtly true. The thing I enjoyed most about chasing it was its solidity. Silence numbed by chain-smoking cigarettes or playing records allowed me to relax.

Sometimes, it felt like I'd be able to shape my destiny by using the pen in my hand or my laptop, but soon I'd fall asleep and then read what I wrote the night before. The words which looked like gold only a few hours prior looked ugly and trite. And the rejection letters from various magazines only validated my fears.

But when housed in a psychiatric hospital for some time, something about it seemed less fatalistic. My pessimism was waning as my mood swings became less common. Boredom had already taken over my free time. Besides those features, though, writing was something that would never leave my mind. Ideas always swirled within my head. I kept telling myself that one day I'd pick up my laptop and write for hours on end, but instead, I'd watch YouTube videos, look at player stats regardless of what sport, or open a Word document to a blank page and falter at the idea of having to fill several pages.

"Okay," I said, "I gotta try something."

"Great," she said. "This is progress, Drew. Major progress."

Afterwards, the nurses summoned some of us to the arts and crafts room. It looked like a normal elementary school classroom. Paintings hung from a clothesline in the back of the room. Apple stickers with adjectives written on their red skin were stuck to the bulletin board on the wall. We all sat down at one of the four oval tables stationed around the room. Leighton sat next to me. We were the only ones at the table. Helen walked to the front of the room while everyone continued to take their seats. The group only held five of us. The others went to their group therapy sessions with Dr. Phillips. I saw the man wearing his usual beanie at the other end of the room. The cigarettes in his hat looked slightly crushed like he accidentally fell asleep on them. He turned to the empty seat next to him with his index finger pressed to his lips as he tried to get the invisible entity to stop making him laugh, but he only cackled louder.

"Okay peanuts, today we are going to do something I call psychiatric art. Everyone, draw a face. And then, I want you to draw smaller faces of every emotion you have felt in the past week," Helen said. She then walked around the room giving out sheets of drawing paper and dull, colored pencils.

"What're you gonna draw for the faces?" I asked Leighton.

"Typical ones," she said.

"Okay cool. I'm not alone," I said to Leighton's amusement.

I was never much of an artist. I knew how to draw a face, but I looked over periodically at Leighton's drawings. Short bursts of pencil hit her paper and she quickly sketched a face, shading in certain areas to create the illusion of it possessing large dimples and a cleft chin.

"That's really good. I didn't know you were an artist," I said.

"Thanks," she said.

"How long have you been drawing?" I asked.

"Awhile, I used to work in Bryant Park, drawing portraits of people and stuff," she said.

"Really?" I asked. "That's awesome."

"Yeah, it was nice in the summer. In the winter, I tried to send some of my stuff to galleries and exhibits, but I never got in," she said.

"You will eventually," I said.

"Thanks," she replied.

I watched while attempting to follow her lead, but my face was a circle with oval eyes and a squiggled 'W' for a bottom lip with a slightly curved line to make up the top one. I looked over and saw her created face. It looked just like her without any hair, possessing soulful eyes and small lips. She guided her pencil across the paper, which made that sweet sound I'd heard whenever I wrote in script using a pen.

"Who's your favorite artist?" I asked.

"Monet," she said.

"Garden at Sainte-Adresse," I said.

"You know that painting?" she asked as she turned to face me.

"Sure," I said, "I did a project on it in high school. I saw it in the Metropolitan Museum."

I was lucky that Monet resonated. My knowledge of art history was poor and though it may have seemed to her like I knew some, I felt strange pretending to be something I'm not.

"I used to go there when I was younger," she said. "Do you have an artist you like?"

"I remember Monet from school, but I don't know much more than the basics. I'm more of a reader," I said.

"I had a feeling," she said.

"Why do you say that?" I asked.

"I saw you reading Bukowski in the common room," she said. "Ham on Rye?"

"Yeah, you read it too?" I asked.

"Yeah, I really liked it," she said.

This shocked me. Chapters were dedicated to Henry, the main character, learning about his bodily fluids through jerking off into a test tube, not to mention his disjointed relationship with his overbearing father and an older woman who seduces him.

"That's a surprise," I said.

"Why?" she asked.

"It's kind of..." I paused, "graphic, I guess, is the best word," I said.

"Art can be just as graphic," she said.

"Fair. Never thought about it that way," I said.

"Do you write?" she asked.

"Not very well," I said.

"Do you do it often?" she asked.

"Reminds me of Dr. Phillips's conversation," I said.

"She did the same thing to me. I couldn't finish a single piece for the first two weeks I was here, but she started making me come here every day and giving her finished pieces," she said.

"She wants me to write something," I said.

"What's it gonna be about?" she asked.

"No idea," I said.

"I'd love to read something you have," she said.

I looked at her and smiled, but my grin didn't conceal the anxiety building in my stomach.

"I don't know. I think it will bore you to tears," I said.

"No, it won't," she said.

"I don't know," I said.

I looked at Leighton and her eyes stared back into mine. The sorrow she felt was palpable and I didn't want her to be doing this out of pity. I wanted to speak, but she beat me to it.

"How about this? I give you a piece of my work and you give me a piece of your writing," she said.

"I don't know. I don't think mine will compare. Just based on this," I pointed to her paper, "I don't hold those odds in my favor."

"I doubt that," she said.

"I would if I were you. I'd love to see your stuff though," I said.

"Only if I can see yours," she said.

I sat silently for a few seconds and considered my options. I thought about the drawer at home filled with stories and ideas no one would ever see. I didn't want to be rude to Leighton, but I also didn't want to humiliate myself either. Leighton's eyes and cute smile, however, imparted a sense of confidentiality that lessened my trepidation, but I still had my doubts. I suddenly remembered those words I'd told Dr. Phillips in her office.

The words 'I gotta try something', brewed in my head and told my brain to stop dissecting every possible path.

"Okay, deal," I said.

Chapter 13

That night, I sat at my desk in my room while the others watched The Iron Giant.

I stared at the notebook beneath me, reading through old journal entries and story ideas I'd never finished. Doodles of a sketched face and a rose with thorns that could be misconstrued as child's artwork made me chuckle.

A few cigarette holes were burned through the written pages. I remembered them. Nice, quiet evening smokes that turned into angry tirades of self-pity.

I finally opened to the next page devoid of ink. I grabbed the dull pencil and wrote my name. It felt strange in my hand as if I was re-teaching myself how to write longhand. I stood up and paced around the room with ideas sputtering around my head. I always started feeling like Hemingway until I realized that my writing was complete and utter shit. I thought about memories, things that had happened to me or things I'd heard. I tried to avoid the recent memories. Every therapy session and the permanent reminders on my wrists were enough to never let me forget. I just wanted to think about something else.

***

Constant Reminders

Ned Crowley sits at a barstool, throwing chips from the party mix at his mouth, missing most of the time. The bartender walks over to the light switches behind the bar and flips them upward. The overhead lights shine brightly, illuminating the wood bar top covered in spilled liquor. Ned continues eating the complimentary chips without noticing everybody around him dispersing through the doors outside.

"Hey, bud, it's 4:00. We're locking up now," the bartender says.

Ned acknowledges him by nodding his head, though his neck is barely able to support it anymore. His friends have long since disappeared, either with a girl for the night or to the bar across the street after the DJ stopped playing music.

Ned finally looks around and sees a beer sitting on the bar. He reaches over and feels its weight. It feels heavy enough and he tries to suck it down in one gulp. The beer spills onto his cleanly shaved chin, but he doesn't care. He's too drunk to care at this point. Jameson shots followed by car bombs followed by LITs left him in a state of confusion with a great sense of humor. He'd been dancing in the middle of the bar with his button-down shirt flung wide open, revealing his chest hair to everyone nearby, but since the DJ stopped, he'd been sitting at the bar. He feels a hand on his shoulder and turns just as he picks up the bottle again.

A large, bald man wearing a black long-sleeved shirt and black pants is standing behind him. He is nearly ten inches taller than the Ned.

"Time to leave, chief," he says.

"I'm good, bruh. One, one, more beer," Ned says and tries to take a swig.

"No more drinks for you, brother," the bouncer says.

"Ah, fuck you," Ned says.

The bouncer grabs him by his shirt and drags him to the front door. Ned knocks the beer over on the bar before the bouncer pushes him into the street. Ned staggers before he falls to the ground. He winces for a moment when his hands don't catch the sidewalk quickly enough so his face hits first.

He feels a cut on his head while he tries to regain his balance but dizziness causes him to fall again. The next time, the spins cease and he stands successfully. He feels the cut and sees some blood, though there isn't much and he laughs out loud while a couple passing by try to hide their faces.

Ned starts to walk, crossing his feet over one another as he sways back and forth, more so when the wind picks up. He walks down the dimly lit street full of college bars that reek of cigarette smoke and dried vomit. Neon signs flicker in the night, temporarily misspelling every masthead name.

After a ten-minute walk during which he lit two cigarettes on the wrong ends, he finally reaches the pale cement leading to the *front door of his apartment complex. Bushes line the path and Ned has made a re-occurring pattern of puking into them.*

Today, he favors the right-hand side and coughs until a stream of liquid pours from his mouth like a sprinkler head.

Afterwards, he reaches the door and tries to pull his wallet from his khaki pants' pocket. He reaches it and tries to open it quickly, only to send it flying in the air. His license, debit card, college ID card, gift cards, and taxi service coupons fall to the cement.

Ned picks up the ID card and pushes it into the black entry box which buzzes as he picks up his loose contents. With his hands awkwardly juggling the cards, he can't find the balance he needs to put them back into their respective holsters. He shuffles to the elevator with the array of cards stuck in between his fingers. The doors open immediately after he presses the up arrow and he staggers inside. He looks for the third-floor button and accidentally presses the second before getting it right. The door closes and Ned leans against the wall and sees his reflection appear on the steel doors. He sees his blonde hair and realizes he was wearing a Patagonia hat to start the night.

The doors finally open and Ned exits the elevator before realizing it's the wrong floor. The door shuts in his face and he decides to utilize the stairs. Twenty steps never looked so demanding, but Ned carries on. Four steps in, he realizes his left boat shoe is missing.

"Ah fuck you," he says aloud and continues climbing the steps.

He sees the door to his floor and uses his shoulder to open it. His apartment door is only a few steps from him, but again, he drops every card he'd been juggling. He leans down and nearly face plants into the carpet, but manages to scoop up his ID card. He holds it against the black detector next to his door. A green light flickers and Ned pushes open the door. With his naked foot, he kicks the cards on the floor into his foyer.

He checks the floor once more with his wandering eyes. The light from the hallway illuminates the foyer where his cards lay on a carpet mat. Ned is satisfied when he sees his license and debit card. He flicks a switch on the wall nearest the door, making the living room visible. The silence is a nice surprise. He remembers his roommates left the bar with their girlfriends and assumes they went to their places.

Ned takes his lone shoe off and curses himself out loud again. He takes off his button down and drops it onto the floor so only his pants are remaining. He unstraps his belt and throws it onto the couch that is surrounded by two lazy boys and a television set. He reaches the kitchen and sees the reminder board hanging from the wall. The marker is attached by a string to the side. Ned bites the cap off and spits it out over his shoulder. He writes a drunk reminder on the board which says: 'Stop doing this'.

***

Ned wakes up in his bed with his head throbbing. The light from the window next to his bed shines brightly and Ned squints at the sun. He looks around and sees his clothes on the floor. Books are also sprawled across the floor while empty pizza boxes lie on his desk though he doesn't remember ordering food. He reads the clock on his phone, which is vibrating on the nightstand next to the bed. It reads '3:24 P.M.'.

He ignores the incoming group messages as his attention turns to the glass of water with a post-it attached to it sitting on the nightstand. He reaches over and grabs it. The note says 'For when you wake up'.

Ned feels the particles of the party mix chips and pizza slices coating his teeth. Without hesitating, he chugs from the glass before violently spitting it out. He gags over the trashcan between the bed and the nightstand. His movement causes some of the vodka in the glass to spill onto his sheets.

When he finally stops gagging, he turns back to the drink in his hand. He sees a glimmer of ink lightly showing from the other side of the post-it. He peels it off and flips it over. The backside of the note reads 'Fuck you. Drunk Ned'.

***

The next morning, the alarm sounded and I woke up in a better mood. I slept through the entire night without a single dream that culminated in me covered in sweat. The door was closed and the lack of a person sitting in the frame made me smile. I liked the solitude of the empty room and what sounded even better was taking a shower behind a closed curtain. I got out of bed and heard a knock on my door. The door opened quickly and Lucky appeared.

"Morning, Drew, just checking to make sure you're awake," he said.

"Is that what usually happens?" I asked.

"Yeah, get used to it," Lucky said with a smile before closing the door.

I grabbed a fresh set of clothes, my toothbrush, toothpaste, soap dish, and shampoo bottle.

It was strange walking around without eyes constantly following me. I didn't even know where to get a towel from being that one of the nurses who'd accompany me to the bathroom always brought it. I left my toiletries on my desk and walked barefoot to the nurse's stand in the common room. Helen stood behind the sliding glass door writing something on a piece of paper. She saw me approaching in my T-shirt and gym shorts. Her red lipstick matched her red hair. The wrinkles on her face made her seem elderly, but she looked healthily skinny for an old woman.

She smiled and slid open the glass window.

"Morning, Drew," she said. "What can I do you for?"

"Morning, Helen. I was wondering where I could get a towel and those plastic sleeves?" I said.

Helen laughed.

"Don't know where to go yet?" she asked.

"Yeah, I'm used to being brought everything. Now I'm lost without you guys," I said.

"I got you covered," she said.

She turned around and walked into the back room. Her wrists flicked as she passed through the open door while her silver earrings glistened from the light bulbs above. She came out a few seconds later holding a blue towel slung over her forearm and two plastic sleeves.

"Here you go, sweetie," she said.

"Thank you," I said.

I sniffled once and felt my nose start to run.

"No trouble at all, darling. Oh here, take some Kleenex, honey," she said and held a small packet of them out to me.

"Thank you again," I said as I grabbed it.

I walked back to my room and grabbed my toiletries. Carrying on to the bathroom, I found a few of the others. Sammy and Otis stood at the bathroom sinks brushing their teeth. Moisture had accumulated on the mirror disrupting the images it was reflecting. Jared walked out of the shower wearing just a towel around his waist.

"Someone give me a fuckin' towel. My head's still wet," he said.

"O-o-o-okay," Sammy said and ran his towel over to him.

"Ain't mean a used one, Jack," he said.

"My-my-my-my na-na-name is Sam-Sam-Sammy," Sammy said.

"It's an expression, jack off," Jared said.

"O-o-ok-okay, y-y-y-yes. I her-her-heard-d-d tha-tha-that be-fo-fo-re," Sammy said.

"Newbie," Jared turned to me, "gimme that towel."

I looked down at my hands.

"I need to shower," I said.

"I need it more than you," he said.

"Get another one," I said.

I was surprised by my response. It was unusually strong. It felt more assertive and grounded. I'd learned his behavior wouldn't lead to a fight. He lived too easily in here. His occasional fits of rage would only spur in the days he felt he had not been worshiped as a saint, and those usually only involved yelling.

Three days ago, he'd launched into a tirade about how the pills he was taking were causing him to break out, ruining his perfect skin.

"I need one now. My skin'll get all dry," he said pointing to his bald head.

"Just get one from the nurses' station," I said.

"I ain't going all the way there, just gimme your towel," he said.

I opened the stall door to my shower and broke eye contact with him. I put my toiletries on the small rack beneath the shower nozzle and hung my clothes and towel up before turning my attention back to Jared.

"Get another towel, I'm using this," I said and closed the door, locking it quickly.

"Piece of shit, open up," Jared yelled and ran to my stall.

He tried to pry the door open, but the lock held firm.

"Goddamn it," he yelled and gave the door one final kick before walking away.

As he did I heard him yelling, "Get outta my way," followed by the sound of toothbrushes and deodorant cans hitting the floor.

I poked my head out of the stall and saw Sammy help Otis pick up his belongings.

"Sorry, I got him angry," I said.

"It-it-it's o-o-o-okay. He-he-he's all-all-always-always ang-angry," Sammy said.

"Does he ever shut up?" I asked.

"No. Guy talks more than the voices in my fucking head," Otis said.

I chuckled and turned back to the shower nozzle. I almost forgot to lock the door behind me. A peculiar feeling arose and I waited for Natalie, Olga, or Helen to caution me about their eternal surveillance, but nothing happened.

I stood for a moment, just waiting until I reminded myself that I was no longer being monitored. An excited spasm gushed through my body causing my muscles to tighten. I undressed quickly, slipped on my protective sleeves, and closed the sliding plastic door behind me. I stood comfortably under the hot water, without the fear of nurses seeing my penis or the hair on my ass. I pissed into the drain and listened to it gargle through the pipes. I sat on the shower floor and let the water fall on top of my head without worrying about any of the nurses who wanted to eat breakfast. My internal clock still waited for someone to barge in for my fifteen-minute checkup, but I knew no one would show.

I dried myself off afterward and got dressed. I walked out with my dirty clothes, my towel, and toiletries in tow. I saw Dougie standing near the sink, removing the wastebasket and dumping its contents into a large garbage can that sat on his trolley.

"Morning, Dougie," I said as I put the wet sleeves into the trashcan.

"Morning, Drew," he turned to me.

He wore blue scrubs over a white T-shirt.

"Hey, this is a silly question, but where do I put dirty clothes and towels?" I asked.

"Off the watch, huh?" he asked.

I nodded.

"Nice, good to see you're getting better. I'll take your towel. You can leave your clothes in your room. Once we do room checks while you're at breakfast, I'll put them in the hamper," he said.

"Okay, thanks," I said and handed over my towel. Dougie placed it in the hamper that rested next to the garbage can.

"No problem," Dougie said and smiled.

I left the bathroom and returned to my room. I placed my toiletries back in their respective places in my armoire before going to my desk. My notebook was the only item sitting on the desktop.

I opened my notebook to where I'd left the pencil sitting in the spine between two pages. I peeled the pages out and tore off the perforated edges dangling like barbed wire atop a fence. I read the pages again, disappointed by the clumsiness of the prose. They sounded better the night before. I stopped thinking right then and there. If I didn't, I knew I would never bring it to Dr. Phillips.

I lined the pages up vertically and with two pounces on my desk, the three holes of each piece of paper aligned perfectly. I slipped on my borrowed moccasins and went to Dr. Phillips's office.

I knocked on Dr. Phillips's door. She opened it while holding a bottle of orange juice in her free hand.

"Yes, is everything alright, Drew?" she asked.

"Oh yes," I said, "I didn't mean to alarm you. I'm just here to give you this."

I handed her the pages in my hand. She took them from me and glossed over the first page. A smile formed on her face.

"Sorry, I didn't mean to disturb you. I just thought if they were in my room any longer, I might burn them or something," I said with a nervous chuckle.

"Don't be sorry, I'm glad you came. I'm gonna read it now. Come back when you're done with breakfast, say 8:15-ish," she said.

"Okay," I said, "I'll be there."

Chapter 14

That day, they served bacon, egg, and cheeses. It sounded great in theory, but thinking about my latest work sitting under the eyes of someone I didn't know very well made the closest thing I'd seen to real food in two weeks nauseating. 'Pipedreams' was the only word that came to mind. I didn't have anything other than myself and a useless hobby that needed doctored courage for me to actually do. I could only watch the clock's skinny hand run itself around the inside of the number arrangement.

Harlan sat across from me at the table.

"You alright?" he asked.

"Yeah, just waiting for this next appointment," I said.

"Anything you want me to hear?" he asked.

"Nah, I just gave her something of mine," I said.

"What'd you give her?" Harlan asked.

"I, uh, I wrote something. She's reading it now," I said.

"Now as in?" Harlan pointed up at the ceiling where her office was.

"Yeah, right now," I said.

"I didn't know you write," he said.

"More like scribble, but it's nothing worth sharing," I said.

Harlan took a sip from his milk carton.

"You said you couldn't play guitar," he said.

"Yeah, I can't really," I said.

"You can though, that's all that matters," he said.

"I guess, but I'm not much good at that either," I said.

"I wouldn't bet on that," he said.

"Why is that?" I asked.

"People who talk about themselves being good at something usually aren't as good as they say, but people who are truly good try to play it off as a hobby since they don't want to make it seem like they really care enough to pursue it," Harlan said.

"Where do you find this shit?" I asked.

"I've been here awhile," Harlan said.

Silence followed Harlan's words and I looked down at my food.

"Where's Leighton?" I asked.

I turned my head and scanned the cafeteria, but I couldn't find her.

"I don't know. She might not be feeling well or something," Harlan said. "When's your appointment?"

I looked at the clock and then turned my attention back to him.

"A few minutes, I better go," I said.

"See you after," he said.

I walked up the stairs and reached Dr. Phillips's room at 8:16. Upon knocking on the door, she quickly opened it.

"Drew, please come in," she said.

Dr. Phillips sounded excited though her outward demeanor remained calm. The sapphire ring on her middle finger dazzled on her dark hand. Her white overcoat hid a blue suit while her heels clicked against the floor on the way to her desk.

"I finished reading your piece," she said.

"I know it's not great, but it's something. A start at least," I defended myself immediately.

"I beg to differ. I think it's good," she said. "Why do you think the opposite?"

"I don't know. It seems clunky and silly," I said.

"It is silly. It's a very funny story. It's well-written and I know you haven't written anything in months. This is good, Drew," she said.

"I guess," I said.

"Why don't you believe this is progress?" she asked.

"I don't know. I guess since I wanted to make a career out of it, but it always seemed like a fantasy," I said.

"Does this have something to do with your father?" she asked.

"Probably. He never liked it much. My mom was a writer, but she passed away when I was twelve. After that, he didn't like the sound of me wanting to become a writer. Well, even before she died he probably didn't like it," I said.

"Why do you think your father felt that way?" she asked.

153

"My mom was a great woman with horrible taste in men. My dad thought, well, thinks that men need to provide and women need to uphold the home front. My mom was a great mother. She never made much money writing though she devoted a lot of time to it. I think my dad thought her hobby was a waste of time since there were no fruits of her labor and he thought she should be doing other things around the house," I said.

"Drew, who cares what your dad thinks?" she asked me.

"I know I shouldn't be as bothered by it as I am. I mean, I know he's an asshole, but he's still my dad. I'm from his seed. His opinion always affected me," I said.

"You know, my dad wasn't in the picture when I was a kid. He left me and my mom before I was born and I always felt guilty. I thought he left because of me, but my mother would always tell me I should never feel that way. She told me to chase what I wanted. I learned later on that my dad couldn't control my life because it was mine. If I didn't try to do what I'm doing now, I wouldn't be here. This life would've been a 'could've been'," she said.

"I think about becoming a writer all the time, but I always feel like I'll never be able to accomplish it," I said.

"Don't say that," Dr. Phillips said. "Because you'll never accomplish anything if you don't try. You don't want to look back at your life and wonder what could've happened."

"But if it doesn't work and reality kicks in, I don't think I can cope with that," I said.

"How do you mean?" she asked.

"If writing doesn't work, I can't work a nine to five job sitting at some desk all day. I can't have a douchebag boss. I'll lose my mind, but I'm stuck in this hole of having no confidence in my writing yet I don't know what the hell I am gonna do without it," I said.

"The only thing I can say, Drew, is you have potential. You are talented and while I cannot promise you accolades or success in your future, I do know that if you never try, I can promise you will never have a chance of succeeding," she said, repeating her wisdom from the day before.

"I know, I just don't know what to do," I said.

"Write about you, about this, about anything you want. Just write every day," she said.

I nodded at her and a desperate grin spread across her face. "Every single day," she said.

* * *

Afterward, I walked to the bathroom. I felt my stomach tremble with a combination of excitement and a full bladder. Touching base while being in a psychiatric hospital was something I found to be contradictory. Being surrounded by walls with others who were deemed mentally ill or unfit to survive in the outside world was an other-worldly experience, but it did give me perspective.

I learned my reality was unlike most and I had a feeling that after this place was over, it would be a highlight in my life, if not the most memorable thing I ever encountered. It gave me a ravenous desire to write.

As I reached the men's bathroom, I heard a faint sound from the women's bathroom on the other side of the hall. The sound grew louder once I stopped walking. It sounded like someone was crying, but I couldn't fully tell. I walked over to the door and leaned my ear against the wood frame. The screams were muffled behind cupped hands, but I could hear the pain. I thought for a moment about opening the door. Knowing my luck, I'd look like a peeping Tom. Someone would turn the corner and demand to know what the fuck I was doing peeking my head into the women's bathroom. The wails got worse though and I felt I couldn't stand still much longer. The common room was slightly busy with patients returning from breakfast and so I calculated the right moment before nudging open the door and walking in.

Leighton sat with her legs extended outward on the bathroom floor. Her hands covered her face while she sobbed into them.

"Leighton?" I asked.

"What're you doing in here, Drew?" she asked.

Her voice sounded frightened.

"I'm not trying to barge in, I just heard you from outside. I wanted to make sure you were okay," I said.

She didn't respond. She just cried harder into her hands. Her eyes filled with water and her dirty blonde hair covered most of her face. She covered her nose to inhale the loose snot.

"You can come to my room and talk about if you want," I said.

I didn't know what to say. It sounded right in my head, but the second the words spilled out of my mouth, I immediately regretted them. I thought she was going to jump down my throat for thinking I could comfort her.

Instead, she sniffled and started to get off of the floor. Her flip-flops landed on their soles and her body rose without my help.

"Would you mind?" she asked.

"No, not at all," I said.

My nerves started to quiver in my stomach and I wished they'd disappear. I wasn't great at consoling. I'd often wallowed in my own misguided hole of self-pity and hatred. I'd never attempted to have real conversations outside of my small circle where trustworthiness did not need to be earned, it was simply a given. Breakdowns in psychiatric wards can be over things as small as missing buttons, but with Leighton, I knew it was something larger than that. It was deeply personal and that scared the shit out of me.

We reached my room quickly, avoiding the orderlies and nurses standing in the common room. Leighton ran in first and I quietly shut the door behind her. She walked over to my bed and sat on the edge.

"What's going on?" I asked.

I didn't even know how to start the conversation. I saw Leighton lean to her left. Her right hand rolled up the sleeve of her black hoodie. As she pulled it up, I could see small blood stains on her skin from skinny cuts. Band-Aids were placed in some places while others were left bare. It looked painful, her arm boasting multiple cuts that looked like a tick-tack-toe board.

"What happened?" I asked though I knew her answer.

I didn't want to jump to any conclusions though.

"I cut myself," she said.

Her voice was hidden behind wheezes and gulps that were working hard to hide her pleading cries for help.

"Why?" I asked.

"I hear them sometimes," she said.

"Who? Your foster parents?" I asked.

She'd talked about them before in group therapy. I never wanted to ask her about them. She didn't ask about why I was there either. Although she'd heard me mention my anxiety and depression, I never dove into my familial problems. I hid those facts for when I was alone with Dr. Phillips. I believed Leighton did the same.

"Yeah," she said.

"What happened?" I asked.

"I had a dream about them last night," she said, but her desperate attempts to catch her breath interrupted the words.

"You wanna talk about what happened?" I asked.

"I don't know," she said.

"I'm not gonna tell anybody if that's what you're worried about. I'll listen if you want me to," I said.

Leighton didn't speak, but instead pulled up her shirt, exposing her tan stomach. I walked over with my head slightly tilted to examine what she was showing me. A scar ran down the left side of her torso. The skin boiled over like a burn, but the jaded scrapes of stabbed flesh told me it was from something sharp. Tears dropped down to the floor from Leighton's face. Some tears were caught by her sweatshirt, but others plummeted down and landed on the cold tile below.

"I'm so sorry," I said.

My voice cracked slightly. I cupped my mouth, sure that my eyes reflected the feeling of shell-shocked bewilderment. Leighton let her shirt fall down so it hovered above her shorts. She started to cry harder. She muffled her sobs with her hands, but I could still hear the wrenching gulps of breath. I took a second to breathe and stopped thinking about reacting. Instead, I bent down in front of her and let her eyes meet mine. Her hands left her mouth and wrapped themselves under my arms. She leaned her face into my chest and cried. I hugged her back tightly and just stood while she poured out her agony. I felt the coldness of her tears through my shirt and my lips started to tremble. All I could do was let her weep.

She started to regain her composure after a few minutes though spliced in between every few breaths were short gasps of despair. I let her go once her grip lessened and it felt acceptable to do so. I grabbed the pack of tissues on my desk that Helen had given me earlier and handed it to her. She blew her nose into one tissue and looked at me through teary eyes, the hazel in each shining brightly.

"You okay?" I asked.

"Yeah. Must seem pretty weird right now, huh?" she said as she sat on the edge of the bed again.

"Not at all. Sometimes people need a shoulder," I said.

"I don't want to bug you," she said.

"I'm here if you want to," I said. "It's fine. Really, I swear."

My mind wore fragile. Words would only do so much, but when everything comes crashing down, sometimes you need an escape. I worried that I'd taken her alone time. The bathroom, though a public space, was a good place to go when you wanted to get away, especially when everyone was at breakfast and the orderlies were searching everyone's rooms. The women's bathroom wouldn't have been populated, but the moment I heard her, I couldn't avoid it. It would have nagged at me like my father's voice.

"Sorry I barged in on you," I said, "I heard you and didn't know what to do."

"No, don't apologize," she said, "I was actually worried about one of the nurses walking in."

"Why?" I asked, "They would try to comfort you too."

"I'm not crazy," she said. "I don't want to be seen that way. Sometimes crying just helps. I get tired of talking to people in lab coats."

"I know what you mean," I said.

I thought of something that could make her feel better as she sniffled into a tissue. Before I said anything, though, she looked down at my hands from across the room.

"How do your wrists feel?" she asked.

I was baffled by the sorrow she felt for me, even though she was the one who seemed more distressed that anyone in the wing.

"Good. Battle wounds I can lie about later on," I said.

Leighton laughed, but mucus in her throat caused her to snort accidentally. She stopped and looked at me with embarrassment before we both burst into laughter.

I looked at her, her white teeth gleaming while the tears evaporated. Her hair swung freely and beautifully as her head rolled from side to side. We finally collected ourselves, and she gave one last gasp before rubbing her eyes. She had a great complexion and her face revealed a certain beauty that I'd never truly seen before.

Leighton was her own person, not mangled by others, but well kept within her own consciousness. Her desires were true and her personality was sincere.

"Uh," Leighton moaned before she took a few deep breaths.

"A good cry helps sometimes," I said.

"Yeah, that it does," she said.

She stood up from the edge of my bed and walked towards me.

"What's up?" I asked.

Leighton extended her arms and wrapped them around my body.

"Thank you," she said.

I hugged her back. We embraced each other since, in that moment, we were all we had. When we mutually released each other, Leighton looked me.

"Quick question," she asked. "Is that it?"

I followed her pointed finger to the notebook sitting on top of my desk.

"Yes," I said glumly.

"Wait here," she said and then trotted out of the room.

I sat back down and looked at the desk. I was stupid to leave it out, but I'd forgotten to hide it in the face of Leighton's predicament. I waited a mere thirty seconds before my door swung open again. Leighton came in holding a piece of paper which she handed me and then shut the door.

I scanned it voraciously. It was a picture of a girl sleeping, but it was an illusion. The covers were formed through small curvatures in pencil drawn, horizontal lines that made it look like loose leaf. The shape of her body under the covers formed a girl who was lying with her hands in between her knees. She laid on her side so her hair fell onto her pillow. The long, flowing locks were beautifully sculpted, every fiber looked tangible, but when I ran my finger across the paper, it remained flat. The girl's face looked like Leighton, but I knew it wasn't her. Only half of the face was exposed, but it didn't have her high cheekbones or button nose. I noticed her lonesome eye was wide open.

"Who is she?" I asked.

"She was a girl I lived with for a while when I was younger," she said. "She used to lay like that for hours."

"Is that why her eye is open?" I asked.

"Yeah, she laid in bed all day, but she was always awake. We used to bring her food in bed, but she wouldn't eat unless she was alone. I never knew why," she said.

"It's incredible," I said.

"Thanks," she said. "Keep it."

"No, thank you, but I can't do that," I said.

"Sure you can," she said, "I have so many drawings anyway."

"Thank you," I said.

She then extended her hand so it stood palms up near my face.

"I haven't picked one yet," I said, "I don't know if I want to anymore."

"How about this?" Leighton proposed. "You open to a random page and give that one to me. If you really don't like it, just go again."

I took a deep breath and turned my back to her so I was staring at my book.

"Drew, it's going to be fine," she said.

I felt her hand on my shoulder and her voice eased the tense muscles in my neck. I reached with my hand and pried my fingernail into the loose-leaf. I lifted up the cover and let it open slowly. I watched as one single piece of paper swayed back and forth before collapsing onto the left side of the notebook. I looked at the two pieces in front of me.

One was a note sheet I used when coming up with a short story in high school for my creative writing class. The other was fashioned in the center of the page. I immediately remembered the lines. It was a poem I'd also written in high school for the same class. I remembered my sister saying it was good, but I thought she was full of shit. Poetry was confusing for me. I didn't know how to read it nor did I know how to write it. I grew frustrated parsing through the different meanings I found in the words and then pretending like I knew what Rimbaud or Pessoa or Sylvia Plath were talking about. I read through the lines and worried that if I went again, I might land on something worse, so

160

I folded the notebook and gave it to her. My finger showed her where to start and she turned away from me.

"Do you mind if I read it out loud?" she asked.

"I guess not," I said with an embarrassed tone.

"I'm not putting you on the spot. It just helps me read poetry," she said.

"I know, I do the same," I said sincerely, but I wished she would just read it in her head. She cleared her throat as her eyes met the first word at the top of the page.

When should one know
How to do
What others are able to?
Remaining silent through and through
While others let their voices do
What he would like to do
Until darkness falls
And the familiar hue
Of blue walls corners you
Doing to you
What you dislike the most.
When you can't do for you
Silence fills you.
And you hope tomorrow
You can do for whom
Matters the most,
Is that you?

"You wrote that?" she asked.

I nodded.

"Drew, that's beautiful," she said.

"Thanks for being nice," I said.

"No, I'm serious," she said.

I didn't know whether or not I believed her. I smiled at her compliments, but internally, my senses leaned towards the fantasy that she would walk out of my room and laugh herself to sleep that night by how cheesy my writing sounded.

"Can you not tell anybody about this?" I asked.

Leighton continued to stare at me, but her face grew concerned and empathetic.

161

"I won't, Drew," she said.

Her hand touched my arm and I felt tremors running through it causing hers to shake as well.

"You don't have to be nervous around me," she said.

I paused for a moment, but I continued to stare down at the floor.

"I'm sorry. I'm always kind of nervous," I said.

"You don't trust many people, do you?" she asked.

I waited and thought about my answer. I wished I could have said she was mistaken, but she wasn't. I shook my head. Leighton leaned down and peered into my sullen eyes.

"I would never hurt you. I promise," she said.

Chapter 15

A few days later, I walked into the visiting center to meet Riley. I saw her sitting at the same table she'd sat at during her previous visits. She wore a white sweater and a pair of tight jeans. Her hair was neatly done with a few waves layered throughout.

Riley stood up once she saw me. We hugged as we normally did before sitting down across from each other.

"Pierce would kill you if he saw you wearing that," she said, pointing at the Notre Dame logo on my T-shirt.

"I know," I said. "I think that's why I like it."

I beamed while Leighton looked at me with a tragic smile.

"Has he visited you in here yet?" Riley asked.

"No. Why?" I asked.

"I left him a message telling him to come, but he never got back to me," she said, "I don't know when he turned into Dad, but he did."

"I don't mind not seeing him and he probably knows that," I said. "It doesn't matter to me what he thinks. In his view, I'm tainted and there is no changing that, so where the chips fall is where they're gonna lie and if he can't accept that, well then, that's that."

I didn't fully believe those words as I spoke them. It was an easy answer to shield Riley from the painful reality, but I felt it'd be better than telling her that my dismissal from my own family burned deeply.

"Yeah, I guess. I just wish he wasn't such an asshole about it. Anyway, what's going with you? How're you holding up?" she asked.

"I'm good. Got my bandages off and the stitches taken out," I said and held up my wrists.

"I knew something looked different," she said.

The stitches had been taken out the day before and only the scars remained. I turned my wrists over so she could see my cicatrices. Red, discolored skin that looked like poorly re-sewn bed sheets ran down each of my wrists. Riley glided her hand over them.

"How does it feel?" she asked.

"Not bad. They're still a little sore, but it could be worse," I said.

"Better than before," she said.

"Absolutely," I said.

We sat in agreement for a few moments while I touched my blemishes. I could feel Riley looking at me.

"You know, Drew, I'm really proud of you," she said.

"Thanks," I said.

"No, I really mean it. I never had to deal with any of this. I can only imagine what hell you were going through, but I'm really happy to see you're getting better," she said.

"Thank you," I said.

I grinned at her and chuckled. It was good to see her ease back into a certain normalcy. No longer was she looking around the hospital walls with those same eyes I initially had, fearful and disbelieving.

Riley took a deep breath and rubbed her eyes with the back of her hand.

"Please don't cry," I said.

"No, I'm good," she said.

"You sure?" I asked again.

"Yeah, I'm fine," she said with a smile. "So how many days do you have left?"

"I think I have eight more," I said.

"That's nice," she said.

"Yeah, but I have no idea what I'm going to do then," I said.

"Well, me and Brock have an extra bedroom. You're gonna stay with us," she said.

"Thanks, but I want to know something," I said.

"What?" Riley asked.

"Is Dad forcing you to do this?" I asked.

"No. Not one bit," she said. "Brock and I are here for you."

"But what about work? Won't I interfere?" I asked.

"No. You come first," she said, "I might have to go away for a few weeks here and there, but most of it is in the city anyway. And Brock will be around."

"I can probably rent a room in Queens or something," I said.

"With what money?" my sister asked sardonically.

"I saved a lot. I might have to find a job so I can pay for school, but I think I'll have enough for a one bedroom unless…" I said.

"Drew, Drew," she interrupted me and put her hand on mine. She clenched tightly and interlocked our fingers as we rested our hands on the table.

"Stop. You don't need to worry about this. Everything will be fine," she said.

"I don't want to bother anyone," I said.

"Drew, you're not a bother. You're my brother," she said.

I looked at her and nodded which was my feeble attempt at telling her I understood, but I didn't fully buy into that idea. Living with my sister seemed like a solution, but I wondered how everyone I'd meet would react when I went to shake their hands.

"I'm gonna have to explain this to everyone from now on, aren't I?" I asked.

"Fuck everybody else," Riley said. "You don't have to explain it to anyone if you don't want to."

Whenever Riley cursed, I knew she was being serious. Our family tendency to swear hadn't afflicted her, but when she slipped into blasphemy, her words were more potent than normal.

"I guess not," I said.

"Drew, no one needs to know unless you want them to. If you're worried about the scars, say you fell or went to push open a glass door and the glass broke," she said.

I snickered with a toothless smile.

"I think I might use that actually," I said to her amusement.

"Me and Brock have a surprise for you when you get out of here," she said.

"Not so much of a surprise anymore," I said.

"Just wait. I think you'll still be surprised," she said.

* * *

I thought about her surprise through the night. I couldn't even guess what it was. Knowing Riley, it could have been a set of car keys for when I got my license. She didn't care if her bank account ran dry or if her career stalled due to my mental state. Her empathy forced me to make a choice about my future and I decided that when I got out of this place, I would not return.

The next morning, the alarm rang and we were told to meet in the common room. Helen and Natalie had herded us like bulls angrily waiting to be fed. A fold-up table had been set up in the common room with utensils and liters of juice. Dr. Phillips came out of her office in her white coat and black suit. Her stockings made her legs look darker than the skin on her arms or it could have been the black heels that made it seem that way. She walked into the common room and wiped the hair from her face, exposing light bags that had formed beneath her eyes.

"Today, we have a special breakfast planned. It is Otis's final day with us," she said and turned to Otis who was standing at the head of the group. We all clapped and a few high-pitched whistles sounded from the back of the room.

"So, we brought out a special breakfast for everyone. Today is also Otis's birthday, so I'd thought we'd celebrate it here to start the day before he leaves and we..." she said and gesticulated with her arms partially raised, signaling us to finish her sentence.

"Never see him ever again," the group said.

I remained silent, but I grinned as Dougie and Lucky brought out a birthday cake.

"Happy birthday to you," they sang as they set his cake down on the table. We joined in.

"Happy birthday to you. Happy birthday to Otis. Happy birthday to you."

Otis awkwardly walked up to the cake. As we finished the final note, he blew out the candles. Then he turned to us and smiled. His teeth were still showered with coffee stain colors. His loose jeans covered the tops of his lace-less construction boots, but his New York Knicks T-shirt looked brand new.

The wrinkles extending down the long sleeves created a perfect crest as if they'd been folded and left in a package for a while. Dr. Phillips handed him a dull knife. He cut through the vanilla cake, exposing the chocolate center and laid the piece on a paper plate. The rest of us formed a line and waited for Natalie or Helen to cut pieces for us. Dougie had gone into the nurses' station and brought back two more liters of apple juice and plastic cups, which he put on the table next to the cake. Jared came walking out of the bathroom zipping up his jeans.

He saw us congregated around the cake.

"What's all this?" he asked no one in particular.

"We're celebrating Otis's birthday and his last day," Dougie said.

"How come I ain't never got cake on my birthday?" Jared asked loudly.

"Because your birthday hasn't happened yet," Dougie said.

"Why does he get it?" Jared asked loudly again.

"I told you already," Dougie said.

"Fuckin' stupid. It's just a goddamn birthday," Jared told everyone.

He turned around from everybody and walked back to his room, stomping loudly in his boots so everyone could hear him. I turned to see Dougie shaking his head as he watched Jared turn into his room. I then saw Otis sitting on the couch with a vacant seat next to him and went over.

"Mind if I sit?" I asked.

Otis tried to answer with his mouth full, but instead decided to smile and quickly dropped his hand, gesturing me to take a seat.

"Sorry," he said. "Bigger bite than I thought."

I laughed as he sucked down the rest with the help from his apple juice. I took a bite and swallowed quickly before turning to him.

"I didn't know you were done," I said.

"Yeah, me neither. I found out yesterday," he said.

"No treatment clinic?" I asked.

Otis shook his head at me, his dreadlocks swinging with every turn of his neck.

"I wasn't on a treatment program. They told me they felt I was ready to leave and I agreed. So, here I go," he said. I was glad to see his rotten smile. His skinny frame looked healthier as opposed to the skin-covered bones I met when I first got here.

"No more hallucinations?" I asked.

"Here and there. I haven't seen that scary dude in a while," he said.

"That's good. What about Molly?" I asked.

"No, I haven't seen here either, but I've always known they're not real, thank God," he said.

"Congrats," I said. "So what's next? Heading back to the Upper East Side?"

Otis scoffed and smiled at me.

"Nah, man, fuck that. I'm heading down to New Orleans, actually. My cousin has a construction gig lined up down there," he said.

I envied his rebuttal to his upbringing. I was too scared to ever stray far from home, but Otis seemed like the type that could go anywhere without doubting his ability to adapt.

"What about you? You only got a week left, right?" he asked.

"Yeah, man. I'm moving in with my sister in the city," I said.

"Where in the city?" he asked.

"71st between 2nd and 3rd," I said.

"Nice, you should check out Oscar's on 60th and Lexington. It's a nice bar with good food. Check it out," he said.

"Will do," I said.

Otis finished the rest of his cake and swallowed the final gulp of juice in his cup. He put his trash on the ottoman before Lucky appeared behind the couch.

"Hey, Otis, it's time. Your cousin is downstairs," Lucky said.

"Looks like that's my cue," Otis said.

We stood up and I extended my hand to him. His grabbed it and pulled me in tightly.

"It's been fun," he said.

"It was great knowing you," I said.

"You too, Drew," he said.

We let each other go and Otis picked up his trash, discarding it in the garbage can. Dr. Phillips then started to speak.

"Everyone, please say goodbye to Otis," she said.

"Goodbye, Otis," everyone said in unison. We all waved our hands at him. He smiled back.

"Goodbye, everybody," he said.

Otis then turned around and joined Lucky as they walked down the hall on his way to exile. I watched as he smiled with Lucky and laughed so his head tilted back. Happiness had grown within him, despite the needle scars on his arms and his teeth that were the same color as dried leaves. Leighton came over and touched my shoulder.

"What're you thinking about?" she asked.

"Seven more days," I said. "Seven more days."

Chapter 16

Three days later, I sat in the common room, talking with Leighton about her drawings and new ideas that she would sketch in her sketchbook.

I was eager for our daily commitment to sharing each other's work. Hours upon hours, we spent talking about our hobbies that one day would, hopefully, manifest themselves as careers. I'd let her read something I'd written the night before while she'd give me a sketch she was working on. Women swinging sledgehammers into private golf clubs with a sign reading 'Men Only', the legs of a woman wearing high heels and the legs of a child wearing dirty sneakers as they stand next to each other in a deli line. The glass counter display held dishes of food with markers showing the names of each. Tuna Salad next to Greek Salad next to Tossed Green Salad and so forth.

I picked her brain on her influences and listened while she detailed the Realism movement in France following the revolution in 1848. I felt her superiority as she talked to me about Pat Conroy, from his cookbooks to his lesser known works like *My Losing Season*, and J.D. Salinger all the while avoiding *The Catcher in the Rye*.

Her knowledge overwhelmed me. I didn't know whether to ask questions or simply wait for her to speak since it always seemed she could read my mind. Her hair danced across her eyes and her laugh triggered an answering smile from me.

I'd never met someone like her before and I felt the strange new pull of attraction that I'd always tried to avoid. Attraction brought me new worries and a painful reminder that someone could grow closer and possibly hurt me, but meeting someone in a psychiatric ward was slightly different.

This place, navigated by people who either felt worthy of being placed here or those of us who were deemed necessary to be here, were all connected by our presence in the same building.

It was like war veterans reuniting when their hair turns white and their tattoos have morphed into wrinkled green skin or ex-ballplayers who appear at the All-Star game to commemorate the era they played in. It was a certain bond that existed, whether you wanted to be a part of it or not.

Protection and a mutual safety were structured around sharing in group therapy which shackled us together like an emotional chain gang. While none of us knew everything about each other, the recognition of being a psychiatric ward patient was something that was collective. We couldn't judge each other based on the scars we'd inflicted on ourselves or the pills we had to take. I knew Leighton felt it when she willingly cried into my arms. It didn't matter if my face was sheared open by a pair of scissors. We were connected regardless.

"How many days do you have left? Only a couple, right?" I asked Leighton as she stuck her pencil in the spine of her sketchbook.

"Yeah, I'm out of here tomorrow morning," she said.

"How're you feeling about it?" I asked.

"Good. I'm excited to get back to the city," she said.

"I'm moving there too," I said.

"Really?" she asked.

"Yeah, I'm moving in with my sister," I said.

"I thought you lived out here," she said.

"I do, well, I did, but now I'm moving in with my sister," I said.

"How come?" she asked.

"It's a very long and boring story," I said.

"Got a long time before tomorrow," she said.

"It's not something worth telling. I don't want to throw my shit on top of it, especially if you're getting out of here tomorrow," I said.

"How about you tell me when you're out of here?" she asked.

"How so?" I asked.

"Call me," she said.

"I don't have your number," I said.

"I left it in your notebook. The same page as the first poem I read," she said.

"You sure you want to put up with someone like me when you're in the real world?" I asked.

"We've been here, Drew. The real world sounds like a piece of cake," she said.

"I don't know about that," I said.

"How about we find out after we get out of here?" she said.

"Okay," I said.

* * *

My mind wandered towards the day when I would be released. I paced around my room, back and forth for hours that night as I worried about everything that could go wrong.

I sat up in bed when I got tired of walking, but I could barely sleep, waking after a few hours clothed in sweat. My shirt stuck to my body while the hair on my legs felt cold and wet. I rushed to grab a towel and take a shower. I wanted to clean up before Leighton left. I felt the patchy beard on my face. It made me look older and more cynical, but I liked that image. Once I was in the bathroom, I stopped and looked at myself in the mirror.

"Since when do you care what you look like?" I asked myself.

I'd never cared in the past. All of the clothes I owned fit in a small gym bag. I'd always had stubble on my face. My hair was usually a wreck since my philosophy was similar to golf's rule, 'play it where it lies'. I hadn't used a comb since my elementary school graduation. I continued staring at myself, begging to understand why I was so nervous about this even though I knew why. I heard the shuffling of footsteps coming down the hall and turned my head quickly, waiting for the door to open, but it didn't and I returned my gaze back to the mirror.

"Relax, dick. Everything will be fine," I said before going into the stall and taking a shower.

I went back to my room afterwards and waited for the others to go down to the cafeteria. The gothic girls sporting all black clothes and black boots slowly walked their way from the bathroom weight scale through the hallway with Helen and Natalie following behind. I watched until Lucky was the only one remaining in the hallway. He came into my room for the morning check.

"What're you doing, Drew?" he asked.

"I just wanted to say goodbye to Leighton. Do you mind?" I asked him.

Lucky scratched his gray beard.

"You know you should be down in the cafeteria with everybody," he said.

"I know, but I just wanted to see her before she left," I said.

Lucky's shoulders relaxed slightly. He took one deep breath and sighed. A smile overwhelmed his face and his eyes met mine. I watched as he turned back to the door and held it open. His blue jeans and white short-sleeved polo leaned against the wood frame. I stood up and started to walk towards him.

As I passed him, he continued to smile.

"Thank you," I said.

"Don't mention it," he said.

I walked through the hallway to Leighton's door. It was slightly cracked and I knocked lightly trying not to startle her. Shortly after, she opened the door entirely.

"Drew, come in," she said.

"Thanks," I said as I walked past her.

Her room was barren. I saw tape stains on the walls where drawings I had been hung. She was packing a few sketchbooks on top of her clothes in a suitcase. The books were heavily marked with pencil that had faded down into the side of the pages.

"You excited?" I asked.

"Yeah," she said.

Leighton stroked the navy blue, baggy sweatpants she was wearing and folded her arms over her plain white T-shirt as she looked at me.

"So what now?" I asked.

"I see you on the outside," she said.

"Yeah," I smiled.

"And I'll bring some of my drawings," she said.

"You want me to bring some more stories?" I asked.

She nodded with a smile.

"Why do you like reading them?" I asked.

"Because they're good," she said.

"Thanks for being nice. I wish they compared to yours," I said.

She smiled, but it didn't hide her embarrassment.

"This might sound weird, but I didn't think this place would work in my favor," she said.

"Why is that?" I asked.

She smiled at me and walked over. She reached with her arms and hugged me tightly. I did the same back. I felt her kiss me on the cheek and then move her soft lips to my mouth.

"I'm just happy I got to meet you," she said.

"Me too," I said. "Me too."

I went with Leighton and Lucky as they walked down the hall towards the elevator. We walked quietly and I could feel a certain sense that Leighton didn't know how to react to getting released. A chapter in her life had closed. It took a degree of understanding once you escaped the threshold of being a patient and then reverting to 'normal life'. Leighton gleamed with nervous excitement as Lucky opened the doors with his keys.

Once he did, she dropped her suitcase and hugged me once again.

"I'll see you soon," I said.

"I can't wait," she said.

She let go of me and picked up her suitcase. Lucky held the door ajar and smiled at us. I watched as the door closed behind them and Leighton was no longer a psychiatric patient. I smiled for her and cackled out loud. I couldn't wait for the day when that was me.

* * *

I started to walk back down the hallway to use the bathroom before eating breakfast.

As I passed Harlan's door, I heard something fall. It sounded like it shook his dresser violently. I stopped and turned back to his door. I glanced down the hall. The recently power-washed floor shone brightly against the lights overhead. I looked at the nurses' station and saw no one behind the glass. The radiator vibrated against the windowsill, but nothing else sounded until I heard one long breath from inside Harlan's room.

I knocked on the door and waited, but nothing happened. I heard his suede shoes rubbing against the floor and he coughed until phlegm reached his mouth. I debated between calling for help or seeing what Harlan was doing. I chose the latter when I realized he could be looking for something under his bed. I didn't want to jump to any rash conclusions. I knocked on the door and turned the handle. I kept my hand on the door as I pushed it so Harlan would hear the creaking and know someone wasn't just sneaking in.

"Harlan, it's me," I said.

I didn't hear anything except what sounded like his breathing. I finally opened the door entirely and let go so it hit the wall. I saw Harlan laying against his dresser. His arms were lying against his legs, covered in blood from the fresh cuts to his wrists. The blood spewed out like a ketchup packet and covered his jeans all the way down to his suede shoes. His green shirt was spattered with blood as well. I ran over to his side and leaned down next to him. I opened his bureau and found a pile of poorly folded T-shirts. My hands guided my actions as they reached for mid-section of one of the shirts and tore it into two pieces.

"Hang on, Harlan," I said.

"Drew," Harlan said, but I initially ignored him.

I wrapped the fabric around each wrist tying it tightly to cut off the circulation. I saw in between his index and middle finger was a strip of wire, purposefully crafted with sharp edges. Blood dripped from the jagged end.

"Okay, I'm gonna get help," I said.

"Drew, wait," Harlan said.

I froze next to him. His pain didn't reach his face. The horror I witnessed was not shared by Harlan. He seemed calm and relaxed. His face didn't twitch and he smiled when he got my attention. His crooked rows of teeth didn't grimace once he looked at his arms. His arms straddled his lower half gently and looked like they hadn't moved since he let them fall there.

"I'm gonna be okay," he said.

"Yeah, I know you are," I said, sounding stupidly optimistic.

"No, I mean, I won't die cause of these," he said.

"I know," I said.

"No, you don't know. They're running the wrong way," he said.

He lifted his right arm for to me to grab. He let it fall into my arms while I reached under the makeshift bandage and cleared a line of sight in order to see the cut. Blood dripped from his

175

fingertips and onto the floor. His skin was separated by a short gash running across his arm.

"Hospital?" I asked.

"Hospital," Harlan said.

"Why?" I asked.

"Harlan," someone cried from the hall. I turned to see Lucky standing in the doorway. "What the hell happened?"

"He cut himself. His wrists are bleeding pretty badly. Get help," I said.

Lucky darted from view towards the nurses' station where an alarm rang and I heard commotion in the hall outside.

"Why'd you do this?" I asked him.

"Honestly?" he asked me.

"Honestly," I said.

"I like it here," he said.

Lucky came barging into the room with a gurney and more nurses entered as well. Natalie appeared and led me away from the emergency staff who were attending to Harlan.

"What the fuck?" I asked Natalie as she led me to a seat in the common room.

"It's okay," she said. "Let me grab you some water."

Natalie trudged down the hallway. Her pink scrubs swung back and forth as the sound of her sneakers connecting with the floor gave a subtle pop. I sat in the cushion chair bent forward with my elbows resting on my knees while my bloodied fingers rubbed my eyes. I brushed back my hair and saw small strands of brown follicles parachuting down to the floor. I didn't hear the medical staff talking nor did I want to see Harlan getting wheeled out on the gurney. Natalie returned shortly with a plastic cup of water.

Out of the corner of my eye, I saw her dangling it in front of me, but I couldn't hear anything she was saying. My ears blocked out all sound and the only thing I could think about was the direction of Harlan's cuts.

* * *

Dr. Phillips sat me down in her office. I still had Harlan's blood on my hands. I'd tried to wash it off, but it didn't work. My fingerprints were colored red and any object I touched stuck to the dry blood. Dr. Phillips noticed and handed me a small garbage can and a box of wet wipes. I needed eight just to get some of the blood washed from my right hand.

"How're you feeling?" she asked.

Silence followed while I periodically glanced up at the ceiling light and then back at my gory hands.

"I don't know," I finally said.

Dr. Phillips sat down at her desk. Her nostrils breathed silently for her while her tongue licked her puckered lips as she thought of something to say.

"I'm sorry you had to see that," she said.

"It's not your fault," I said.

I dragged the wipes across my hand harder and watched them turn red as if I'd stuck them in cranberry juice. After only a few moments, the trash bin Dr. Phillips had given me from behind her desk was filling quickly with discarded wipes.

"Is he gonna be okay?" I asked.

"Yes. The doctors told me he's stable," she said.

"When can I see him?" I asked.

"He'll be back in two days," she said.

"I leave by then," I said.

"I'll make sure you see him before you go," she said.

"Thank you," I said.

"Did he say anything to you while you were with him?" she asked.

"I don't remember," I said.

I looked up from my hands and met Dr. Phillips's brown eyes. They pulsated with red veins that made her look afflicted. She nodded at me. Silence returned and once I felt I cleaned enough of the blood off, my fingers had already begun to wrinkle. I reached into my pocket and pulled out a cigarette.

"May I?" I asked Dr. Phillips.

She nodded and flipped me a lighter that was sitting on her desk.

"Do you smoke when you're nervous?" she asked.

"I guess. I usually crave them when I'm nervous," I said.

"Why?" she asked.

"Something to do with time, I guess. One cigarette means for two minutes I'm occupied by something else other than what's bothering me," I said.

"What else calms you down?" she asked.

"Writing helps. Leighton helped me too, for some reason," I said.

"She's a good girl," Dr. Phillips said, "I saw you two over the past couple of weeks."

"Yeah, she shared her artwork with me," I said.

"I heard," Dr. Phillips said. "Are you going to continue your contact when you get released?"

"I think so, but I'm not sure," I said.

"Why are you not sure?" she asked.

"I don't trust people too much. I always feel like they're gonna hurt me," I said.

"You know how to find out if people are trustworthy?" she asked.

I shook my head.

"Trust them," she said.

"Hemingway," I said with a chuckle.

We smiled at one another. Dr. Phillips didn't hide behind her lab coat. Her emotions were real, or at least I felt they were. She didn't choose her words or work out vocabulary in her head. She was just giving me details she full-heartedly believed. Her voice remained soft and tender, but underneath there was a firmness, the kind that told me she wasn't bullshitting.

"I know I have to trust people to find out. It's just vulnerability. I don't know why, but it freaks me out," I said.

"Don't worry about anyone else right now. You can open up to others. You choose who these people are, but you can open up to whoever you like. The decision is on you and whether you feel comfortable," she said.

"I only feel comfortable around a select few and two of them are sworn to secrecy by law and the other is biologically related to me," I said.

"You know something, Leighton hasn't shown any of her work to anyone else other than me, with the exception of the things she hung on her wall, and those she didn't even draw while she was here. She's not toying with you, Drew, I promise. She actually enjoys you and trusts you enough to give her something she is passionate about. All I'm saying is you have to try to change your thinking because if you don't, then your progress will stall. That is a certainty," she said.

"I know," I said.

"You've made great progress," she said, "and I don't want to see it stop."

"Me neither," I said, "I'm still working on it, but I know the responsibility is mine."

"Good," Dr. Phillips said. "Change is the key. Just keep an open mind and the rest will follow, I'm telling you. Please trust in me that I'm telling you the truth."

"I trust you," I said, "honestly."

Chapter 17

I could barely sleep the following night. I was excited to leave the ward. Yet one thing lingered on my mind as I paced around my room checking the sky to find the morning light.

"I like it here," I repeated Harlan's words to myself.

The thought of a friendly relationship between this place and myself seemed unimaginable. I didn't want to be there any longer than my treatment required. I wanted to know Harlan's reason.

I closed my eyes for a few minutes before nodding off for what couldn't have been more than an hour. I lifted my head and finally found the early morning lights, pink as the sun slowly lifted through the cloudless sky. I watched birds flap their wings up and down as they glided through the air, never once interrupted by walls or chain link fences. Instead, they just went wherever it was they felt like going. Wind rattled the window as it whistled by. I looked at my pack of cigarettes sitting on my desk. I wished I had a lighter and an openable window. Instead, I sat in my bed and grabbed my lips. I bit at my fingers, tearing off a slab of my overgrown thumbnail and chewing on it until the morning alarm sounded.

Once it rang, I stood up and put on my clothes, including my old, tattered sweatshirt and stepped into my lace-less sneakers for the first time since I'd been admitted.

"Drew," Natalie said as she knocked and pushed the door open simultaneously.

She saw me standing in the center of the room.

"Oh, great, you're up," she said and scribbled something quickly on her clipboard.

"Yeah. Hey, I was wondering if they brought Harlan back today," I said.

"Yes, they brought him in a few hours ago," she said.

"Can I talk to him before I leave?" I asked.

"I don't think that'll be a problem," she said, "Olga is posted at his room right now. I'll let her know you're stopping by."

"Thank you," I said. "And if I don't see you before I leave, thank you for everything."

"Thank you, Drew. Stay safe," she said with a wave before closing the door.

I turned back to my armoire and opened it. My gym bag sat nestled in the bottom underneath the empty coat rack that lacked hangers. I ran my hand through the top shelf, knocking over the partially empty shampoo bottle they'd supplied after my first one ran out. I only felt the toiletries I'd been given when I arrived, and so I closed the doors. I didn't feel like taking anything from the ward except the drawings Leighton had given me.

I wasn't trying to forget my tenure as a psychiatric ward patient, but I didn't want to remind myself of it either, even if it was just the smell of their soap.

I then went to the dresser sitting underneath my bed. I opened the drawers and took out the remaining clothes. I didn't care where they ended up in my bag, just as long as they were in there somewhere.

I went to my desk, grabbed my remaining cigarettes and placed them in my bag. Then, I picked up my notebook and opened it to the green folder resting inside. I opened my desk drawer and found the drawings Leighton had given me. I went through each of them and when I was satisfied I hadn't lost any, I folded them in half and stuck them in the folder. I felt bad about the creases that had formed in the middle of the pages, but I didn't want them to rip in my bag. I wanted to make sure I could hold onto them, whether it meant they were my lasting memory or the first of many. I placed the book on top of my loose clothing.

The final contents were the pair of moccasins Dougie had given me. I grabbed them by the heels and placed them at the bottom of my bag, covering them with clothes so the dirt embedded in the soles wouldn't get all over my notebook and more importantly, so they wouldn't ruin Leighton's drawings.

As I zipped my bag shut, I placed it on the desk chair and took a step back. I scanned the room a few times and checked under the bed and desk to see if I'd forgotten anything, but only dust bunnies and pencil shavings were strewn about on the floor.

I looked back at my gym bag. Those were my only possessions at that moment. No more, but it could have very well been less. I leaned on the edge of my bed and remained there for a moment while I took everything in. It just felt hard to believe that I was ever in here, much less about to be released.

A knock startled me. It lasted slightly longer than I expected.

"Drew, are you decent?" I heard Dr. Phillips ask.

"Yes, I am," I said.

Dr. Phillips smiled as she walked into the room. I heard the morning chatter along with the stampede of the others who were heading downstairs to the cafeteria.

"How're you doing? All ready to go?" she asked.

"Yeah, I'm ready. Feels weird though. I don't really know how to put it," I said.

"I understand. That's normal. Well, I wanted to let you know that your sister is waiting downstairs. Dougie will take you down to the storage room where you can collect your belongings and then after a few forms, you'll be on your way," she said.

"Thank you," I said.

"No problem," she said.

"No really, thank you for everything. I don't know where I'd be right now if it weren't for you," I said.

Dr. Phillips walked over to me and stuck her hand out. Her red lips grinned and a gleam covered her face. Even if I had lied to her in that moment, that look would probably still be plastered to her face, but she had a way of making it feel special.

"Thank you," she said.

"What'd I do?" I asked.

"Three weeks ago, you said, 'There's nothing worth saving here.' Thank you for trusting me to change that," she said. "Do you feel that way too?"

"Yeah. I still struggle at times, but I feel better than I did before. Definitely," I said.

"Struggles occur. That's part of getting better. If you ever need to contact me, I gave your sister my number and here's my card in case," she said.

Inside her lab coat pocket, she pulled out a business card with her name and number printed on it. I nodded my head and smiled. Dr. Phillips's arms wrapped around my shoulders and we hugged.

"I called Dr. Merriweather. He wants to you to call him today at some point to set up a meeting," she said as we let go of each other.

"Okay, will do," I said.

"I'll let Dougie know you're ready," she said as she backtracked to the door.

"Okay thank you, but do you mind if I see Harlan before I go?" I asked.

"Oh right, yes. Olga is expecting you," she said.

"Great, thank you again," I said.

"Take care, Drew, and please, keep writing," she said.

"I gotta come up with some more ideas," I said.

Dr. Phillips stopped moving and tilted her head slightly. Her lips contorted to make a smirk.

"It's all fodder, Drew. Everything you've ever been through or heard," she said.

"I guess so," I said.

"Don't stop writing. It can only help you," she said. "Promise?"

"I won't stop," I said, "I promise."

***

I went to the bathroom afterwards, reminding myself as I stood over the urinal that this was the last time I'd be taking a piss in this building. It made me chuckle. I pulled the handle down on top of the urinal and listened as the water was sucked through the drain before making my way to the sink. My reflection smiled at me, but I couldn't help but think about Harlan sitting in a pool of his own blood.

I walked back to my room. The door was partially opened and I nudged it forward with my shoulder before closing it without ever once looking up from the floor. As I turned towards my bed, Jared's feet bounced against my desk. He sat in my desk chair with my bag on his lap, holding my notebook in front of his face.

"What the hell are you doing here?" I asked.

"Readin'," he said.

I quickly walked over and tried to snatch my belongings from him, but he shifted himself so his feet were back on the floor, ready to lunge at me like some sort of predator. He held my notebook out of my reach with his long arms.

"What is this shit?" he asked.

"None of your business," I said and grabbed his forearm.

He snarled and threw his free hand into my stomach, sending me gasping for air on the floor.

"Don't ever fuckin' touch me," he said as he stood up.

I heard him flicking through the pages of my notebook before shutting it.

"I think I'll keep this," he said. "You ain't need it no more."

I rose to my feet, staggering away from him in case he tried to keep me down.

"Give it back," I said.

"You remember who runs this place? If you leavin', I get something," he said.

"You are delusional," I said with a cough.

"Ain't me. That's you if you thought you was getting outta here without giving somethin' to me," he said.

I don't know what made me do it. Maybe it was the fact that I'd never see him again or maybe because my writing re-entered my life as a focal point of maintaining my health. The only thing I could think of though were Leighton's drawings. I couldn't lose those. She shared those with me and Dr. Phillips. There was a certain duty behind retrieving them. Her drawings weren't for Jared's eyes.

I sprinted at Jared with my head titled forward, aimed directly at his stomach. My hands latched onto his body sending him off balance. One of his feet left the ground and we spun into the desk. I heard my notebook drop to the floor and felt Jared's fists connecting with my ribs. We grappled with each other before he pushed me off him and we both stood firmly. His massive frame had a long reach and I protected myself by keeping my fists up next to my temples. This time, he charged me, but I side-stepped him. I pushed him from behind lightly and his momentum did the rest of the work by sending him into the wall. As I stood watching, he looked at me. His teeth were pressed together tightly. Red blood vessels swam through his eyes while the veins in his forehead popped. This time when he charged, he didn't miss. He wrapped me up like a linebacker and tackled me to the floor, his entire body landing on top of mine.

The hard tile made me yell in agony before I saw his fist raising behind his ear. I put my hands back in their defensive position and narrowly blocked his haymaker. Had it not been for Dougie, I would've most likely ended up in a coma. Dougie ran into the room and tackled Jared off of me before the second wave of punches could be thrown. Lucky followed behind him while Dr. Phillips pulled me up from the floor. She sheltered her arms around me as we walked to the common room. I sat on the couch while more nurses appeared in my room, bringing along with them a gurney that was fashioned with restraints.

It took them a little while before they reappeared in the hallway with Jared tied down to the gurney. He lay motionless as the nurses guided him down the hall. Dougie and Lucky were the last to leave my room. Both fixed their shirts that had been ruffled in the struggle. Sweat dripped from Lucky's forehead while Dougie took controlled breaths that made him seem calmer than his counterpart. Dr. Phillips brought me a cup of water.

"Are you okay?" she asked.

"Yeah," I said.

"What happened?" she asked.

"Went to the bathroom, came back and found him sitting at my desk," I said.

"What was he doing?" she asked.

"Told me he was taking my notebook. Said I didn't need it anymore and he wanted it, so…" I said, shaking my head.

"You fought over your notebook?" she asked. "Why didn't you just come to one of us?"

"Just snapped, I guess," I said. "Leighton's drawings are also in there. I didn't want to lose any of that stuff."

Dr. Phillips smiled at me and titled her head.

"What is it?" I asked.

"I know fighting is never a good thing, but you fought for your work and someone else's too," she said.

"Yeah?" I asked.

"It's progress," she said.

"Progress?" I asked. "I'm not in trouble."

"No, we know how Jared is. But you? No. I know why you did what you did. And I also know that it says more about you than you may realize," Dr. Phillips said, still smirking at me the whole time. "You are finding yourself again and don't let anyone tell you differently."

After our chat, I went back to my room. It was in disarray. The desk had been pushed so it no longer rested against the wall. The chair was overturned. My bag was on its side with the contents spilling out. I found my notebook and turned to the folder. Leighton's drawings were still there, relatively undamaged as were the rest of the pages. It was a relief. I picked up my bag and threw everything back inside, except for my notebook which I placed neatly on top again. Dougie poked his head through the doorway.

"Drew?" he asked. "Everything all right?"

"Yeah," I nodded. "Thanks for saving my ass."

"Don't worry about it. I just want to make sure you're okay," he said.

I started to push the desk back into place, but Dougie stopped me by saying, "Don't worry about that Drew. We'll take care of everything."

"What about my toiletries and shit?" I asked.

"Leave 'em. We'll clear everything out," he said.

"Okay, thank you," I said as I grabbed my bag and walked to the door.

Over my shoulder, I twisted my head around the room allowing my eyes to see if I'd missed anything for the final time, but nothing revealed itself. I turned back to the door, which Dougie held open with his sneaker. I held my head down as I walked past him and only turned when I heard the door close. Dougie flipped through his keys before picking one and locking the door. Room number 26 no longer belonged to Drew Thomas.

"Dougie, do you mind if talk to Harlan for a few minutes?" I asked.

"Please go ahead. Take all the time you need," he said.

"Thank you," I said.

I walked down the hallway and saw Olga sitting outside Harlan's open door. She sat with her chin resting on her coupled sausage fingers. Her blue scrubs looked uncomfortable and wrinkled like she hadn't washed them in days. She heard my footsteps approaching and turned her head without lifting it from her entwined phalanges.

"Morning, Olga," I said.

"Hi," she murmured.

"Can I see him?" I asked.

"Yeah, yeah, I heard already. Go in," she said.

"Thanks," I said. "Do you mind if I close this?"

"Yeah, I mind," she said.

"Never mind then," I said.

I walked into the room and saw Harlan lying in his bed. His eyes were closed, but they opened when he heard my sneakers squeaking against the floor. He sat up. His hair looked greasy and his face looked like it was covered in dry sweat. He hadn't showered in a few days and I could smell it once he slid the covers off of his body.

"Sorry, Drew," he said.

"Sorry about what?" I asked as I pulled the chair from under his desk over to the edge of the bed.

"I didn't mean for you to see that," he said.

"It's okay. How're you doing?" I asked.

"I'm fine, man. Just tired right now," he said and coughed loudly. "What about you? How're you doing? I heard about Jared."

"I'm good. Dougie got there before he kicked the shit out of me," I said.

"God, I hope that's the end of him in this place," Harlan said.

"Yeah, well, if so, you're welcome," I said with a smile.

While he chuckled, I looked at the floor where his shoes were. They were bloodstained from toe to heel. I opened my gym bag.

"What're you doing?" he asked.

"I brought you something," I said.

I pulled out the pair of moccasins and held them up.

"They fit me pretty good so they should work for you," I said.

"Thanks, Drew," he said. "You're leaving today, right?"

"Yeah, I'm on my way out," I said as I put the moccasins on the floor next to his stained shoes.

"Congrats," he said.

"Thanks," I said.

A moment of silence followed as I leaned forward in the chair while he wiped the sweat away from his head with his bandaged hands.

187

"Can I ask you something?" I asked.

"What is it?" he asked.

"Well, I was wondering about the last thing you said to me. You said, 'I like it here'," I asked him in a whisper so Olga wouldn't hear. I coupled my hands together anxiously, waiting for a response.

"How do you mean?" he asked.

I leaned in closer to keep our conversation inaudible.

"You want to stay here?" I asked him.

Harlan sighed and looked down at his hands. He took a few breaths and then he looked at me with a face I cannot forget. It grew long and gaunt. The exterior skin seemed to loosen as if he was telling his muscles not to worry anymore so they could just be instead of positioned a certain way. He licked his lips quickly, wetting them, which minimized the dry skin forming on the corners of his mouth. I could smell his morning breath blowing into my face.

"I don't have anyone out there. I know this life. I don't know that one," he said, nudging his head towards the window.

"You ever think about getting out?" I asked.

"Sometimes, but I'm not ready. I'm not ready to go live on the streets," he said.

"You can always call me," I said, "I'll leave my number with Dr. Phillips if you'd like."

"You don't need to. I'm a weight. I'm not dragging you down with me," he said.

"You're not a weight," I said.

"Yes, I am," he paused, "I'm not meant to be out there."

"You won't know until you try," I said.

"Some of us like not dealing with the consequences of our problems," he said. "Here, I can deal. Out there is no place for someone like me."

I let my head drop so I was staring at my poorly fitted sneakers.

"Hey, hey," he said. "Don't let me bring you down. Go out there and do you, man. I'll be okay in here," he said.

"Can I visit or write?" I asked him.

"Anytime you'd like," he said.

I stood up and Harlan stuck out his bandaged hand. He dangled his fingers towards me. I reached over and grabbed them gently.

"It was great meeting you," I said.

"You too," he said.

"I'll see you soon," I said.

"Thanks, Drew," he said.

Olga grunted as I walked past her. Her eyes didn't follow me, but she knew I would still be able to hear her.

"You guys got me working fourteen-hour shifts, you know that?" she said.

I stopped for a second. Dougie, who'd been waiting in the hallway for me stopped as well. I didn't turn my head and instead looked down at the floor.

"So quit," I said and started walking again.

Dougie walked in front of me to the double doors at the end of the hall. With his key ready, he inserted it into the lock and twisted his hand. I heard the lock release and Dougie opened the door. I couldn't remember what anything looked like past that point. He held the door open for me and I walked past him. I heard the door slam behind me and turned while Dougie pressed the down arrow button on the wall.

"Glad to be going?" he asked.

"Feels strange," I said.

"Better than coming in though, right?" he asked.

"Without a doubt," I smiled.

The elevator chimed and the doors opened. I walked in with Dougie and he pressed the button reading the number '1'. I felt the elevator drop and I quietly thought about Harlan. It was bittersweet leaving, but knowing that he was safe, at least in his own head, helped. I knew the feeling of depression and wanting it to be over. I was glad Harlan didn't show that to me. He seemed content with where he was. The elevator arrived at the first floor where I saw the elevator waiting area I'd entered on my first day. I walked out and followed Dougie through the double doors that led us back into the hallway where the storage room was. He opened the door and I followed him inside.

"Thomas, Thomas, where are you?" he said to himself as he ran his hand up and down the cubbies. "Ah, there you are."

His hand reached into a cubby and pulled out a plastic box with my name marked on it. He peeled the lid off and I found my belt sitting just as it had been when he put it in. I grabbed it and secured it around my waist. Dougie handed me my one of my shoelaces and held onto the other.

"Take your shoes off," he said and extended his hand, "I'll do one. You do the other."

"Oh, thank you," I said and gave him my left sneaker.

We wove the laces in and out of their respective holes like spaghetti. I reached the top of my sneaker at the same time Dougie finished lacing my other one. He gave it back to me and I put them on. The ankle support and tightness fitted my foot well. I tied them loosely and then wiggled my feet with excitement.

"Never thought I'd be so happy to have these crappy things back," I said.

Dougie smiled and looked into the rest of the box.

"Here you go. Your phone and your wallet," he said.

I took both of them and checked to make sure they were exactly as I left them. They were and I put them in my pockets, immediately feeling the strangeness of having anything in them other than a single pack of cigarettes. Dougie next held up several pairs of strings from my gym shorts and sweatshirt.

"You wanna put them back in now or do it later?" he asked.

"I'll do it later. It's fine," I said.

"Okay and lastly, we have the strap to your bag," he said holding out the long, black Nike strap. I grabbed it and hooked it onto the end of my gym bag. I then let the strap hang off my shoulder as it supported the weight of my belongings.

"And that's all," Dougie said.

He turned the box towards him and peeled off the tape spelling my last name. He dropped it into the garbage can residing under the desk and smiled at me.

"Now we can get you outta here," he said.

I followed him back down the hallway to the front desk window where I saw Riley and Brock seated in the waiting room. I saw a woman standing at the counter who smiled at me. I hadn't seen her before. She had curly brown hair and a skinny frame complete with a wide smile.

"Drew Thomas?" she asked.

"Yes," I said.

"Okay, I just need you to sign these forms," she said handing me a clipboard holding several discharge papers. A pen dangled off a metallic silver chain attached to the top.

"Your sister gave me your insurance card, so you're all good there," she said as she watched me sign my name at the bottom of the pages. After the final signature, I stuck the pen back in its sheath and looked up.

"You're all good to go," she said and handed me my insurance card.

"Thank you," I said.

I turned back to Dougie.

"Thank you for everything, Dougie. I really appreciate everything you did," I said and stuck my hand out.

"Drew, it was my pleasure. I hope I never see you again," he said.

"Me too," I said. "Tell everyone I said goodbye."

"Will do. Take care, Drew," Dougie said.

I turned to the door that led out to the waiting room and opened it. Riley looked up from the book she was reading. Her eyes met mine and we both responded by smiling. She ran over to me while Brock followed behind her. She hugged me tightly, twirling me in circles as she laughed.

When she let go, Brock gave me a handshake and a hug.

"It's good to be on this side," I said.

"It's better to have you on this side," Riley said.

Chapter 18

I hopped in the backseat of Brock's Jeep. Everything from putting on a seatbelt to the smell of the car made me giggle.

"This is bizarre," I said.

"What?" Riley asked as she sat in the front seat.

"Everything feels new," I said.

"How're you doing?" she asked.

"I'm fine, why?" I asked.

"Dr. Phillips, is that her name?" she asked to which I responded with a head nod. "She told me one of your friends tried to kill himself."

Brock hopped in the front seat and ignited the car's engine. He turned to me once he realized what we were talking about.

"Yeah, but it's okay," I said.

"No, really. How are you?" she asked.

"I'm okay. He didn't try to off himself," I said.

"What do you mean?" she asked.

"He said Dr. Phillips told him she felt he was making progress and would be able to leave soon, but he doesn't wanna go," I said.

"Drew, he slashed his wrists open," Riley said.

I lifted the sleeves on my sweatshirt and showed Riley my left wrist. I dragged my finger across the skin as if I was measuring the diameter of my wrist and said, "Hospital."

I then drew my finger vertically along the scar that ran up to my forearm and said, "Morgue." Riley nodded her head at me and grabbed my hand.

"You wanna talk about it?" she asked.

"No, not really. Let's just get outta here," I said.

I didn't want to tell Riley or Brock about Harlan or my fight with Jared. It seemed wrong to say anything. I thought it would've made things harder and I was glad to see Riley and Brock in better moods than I'd recently witnessed.

"Okay," she said to Brock and he started to drive. I looked out of the back window as we left the psychiatric hospital building. I heard ambulances circling quickly into the emergency entrance and I watched as the windows that were barred disappeared to the point where they just seemed like empty glass panes. The place I once called my residence slowly shrunk in the distance as we drove farther away. We crossed a bridge elevated above the train tracks below and I lost the sight of the hospital due to an office building obstructing my view.

I turned back to the windshield and met Brock's eyes in the rearview mirror.

"All good back there?" he asked.

"Yeah, I'm good," I said. "I'm good."

It took us an hour and fifteen minutes to reach their apartment on 72nd street between 2nd and 3rd. They parked on the street and I got out of the car, greeted by the smell of the city air, rife with cigarette smoke, gasoline, perfume, and sewage. I grabbed my bag from the trunk and followed Riley and Brock to the front door. We walked on the cracked sidewalk covered by scaffolding to the semi-circled driveway that led to a set of golden doors. A woman passed us with her poodle. Her large sunglasses sat on the top of her white hair as she played with her pearl necklace with her free hand. The dog barked as we walked past, slightly pulling her off balance. We approached a tall doorman who was smiling at us.

"Mr. Mann. Ms. Thomas," the man said with a thick sub-continental accent.

"Hello, Anwar," they both said.

Anwar rubbed his thin goatee quickly, settling the stray hairs back into their square shape.

"Anwar, this is my brother, Drew. He's gonna be staying with us for a while," Riley said.

The pair split, opening a path for me to reach Anwar. I smiled shyly and shook his hand. His typical uniform, a three-piece suit, was neatly dry cleaned and his chauffeur's hat was perfectly aligned on his bald head.

"Nice to meet you, Drew. I'm Anwar," he said.

"Nice to meet you too," I said.

I watched his eyes gaze down at the scars on my wrists and our handshake lasted a few seconds longer than it should have. I immediately pulled each sleeve down so they covered both of my hands entirely.

"Well, great. Do you need anything?" he asked finally.

"No, I, uh, I think we're good," Riley said. "Thank you though."

Anwar led us to the front door. He pulled the golden handle and held the glass frame open for us. We all said, "thank you," as we passed. The floor turned to marble with one black tile for every white one. It looked like an expensive and slightly cheesy chessboard. The sound of Brock's loafers clapping against the floor coupled with the high-heeled boots Riley wore over the bottom half of her jeans echoed throughout the building's first level.

The lobby had a desk to our left where two men stared at a computer screen. Brock waved to one of them who returned the same gesture. As we walked past them, we reached the elevators. Four different shafts were stationed in the narrow corridor. Riley pressed the up arrow and an elevator chimed as its doors flung open. We walked in and Brock pressed the button designated '32'. The elevator moved quickly and the numbers rapidly increased on the digital dial, softly chiming each time we passed another floor. It stopped gracefully and the doors opened again.

I walked out and followed Brock and Riley down the narrow hall. Doors were aligned with the ones parallel. We reached the end of the hall where a lonely door stood facing us. I heard Brock rattling his keys as he shoved one into the lock. He opened the door and I entered their apartment for the first time.

The brown wood floor shone as the sunlight broke over the skyscrapers. I kicked my shoes off on the foyer mat and left them under the small black table that sat below an oval mirror. I entered and saw a doorframe without a door. It led into the kitchen, which had a beautiful granite counter top that converted to a bar on the other side. The cabinets were nicely constructed and colored white. The floor was covered in fake tiles that felt like pressurized rubber. On my left was a short hallway. I saw one door at the end of the hall and another on the right-hand side.

"What do you think?" Riley asked.

"It looks amazing," I said.

"Well, let's show you around then," she said.

She walked past me and I followed behind. On the other side of the kitchen and past the hallway I'd been looking down, there sat the living room.

"This is the living room and dining room," she said.

A black, leather couch sat at the top facing the mounted flat screen residing on the wall head-on. On each side of the couch, two leather chairs faced the television at off-centered angles. Behind the couch, nearest the wall on the other side of the room, sat an eight-person dining table. It was an elegantly crafted piece: the wood's pigment held several slightly different colors that looked like a mixture of different peoples' coffees combined.

Walking past the table, Riley showed me through a door that led out to a small balcony with two chairs and a small table.

"This is the balcony," Riley said. "I love it here."

I looked out and could see over the city. Taxis honked at each other and one man swore his way through traffic, his tires braking quickly followed by a cringe-inducing scraping sound. Birds flew overhead. I watched their wings effortlessly flap until they stopped and then simply glided like a plane. My vision wasn't objected by prison bars or the feeling of confinement I felt in the recreation yard when birds or planes flew overhead.

"This is awesome," I said.

"Yeah, it's great. Come. I'll show you your bedroom," she said.

I followed Riley back inside to the hallway I'd seen when I'd first come in. We walked to the door on the right-hand side. Riley turned the gold knob and flung it open. Sunlight poured in from the three, paneled windows to the left of the door. A bed rested with its post against the wall, facing the windows. A dresser was stationed against the wall across from the door. I looked at the windows and saw a television that looked familiar resting on a nightstand in front of them.

"Is that my television from home?" I asked.

"Yeah. We grabbed it when we went to pick up some more of your things. I put the other stuff in the closet for now," she said and pointed to the sliding door to the right of the dresser.

I went over and opened it. I looked down and saw a duffle bag sitting next to my record player. The records themselves were lined up standing on the floor, resting against the wall for support. The acoustic guitar I messed around with was leaning against the wall as well. I opened the duffle bag and found my laptop with the charger wrapped around it. I found dress shirts and the dinner jacket that I sometimes needed to wear for special occasions. Fresh pairs of socks, my dartboard, and the books I'd left on my bureau that I hadn't finished reading yet were neatly tucked underneath everything. My mason jar filled with guitar picks was tucked in the side pocket. In the other side pocket was a plastic bag holding my journals. All of the loose pages of writing I'd kept since I was in high school were bound together by rubber bands and neatly placed on the floor. I turned around to Riley who was standing with Brock. I guessed he'd appeared while I was busy looking at all of the items they'd collected for me. I walked over to them and hugged Riley. She opened her arm and I did as well to let Brock in.

"Thank you so much," I said.

"Anything for you," they said. "Anything."

We all finally let go and chuckled with excitement.

"Oh, Drew. There is one more thing," she said and pointed with her finger.

I hadn't even noticed the desk and computer chair that sat to the immediate right of the door. I ran my eyes over it and saw a typewriter, a gray Royal, sitting next to a stack of blank papers. I walked over and ran my fingers across the keys. They felt fresh and untouched.

"You didn't have to do this," I said.

"Yes, we did," she said.

I walked back over to her and hugged her as tightly as I could.

"Thank you for everything. You have no idea how much this helps," I said.

I felt tears welling in my eyes and closed them quickly. I hoped they wouldn't dwell, but the moment seemed too beautiful to not have a reaction. Riley was my savior. I had stepped over the edge, but Riley helped me find my way back.

Through fire, Riley would be there and for that, I couldn't help but tear in that moment. She meant everything to me when I thought of the word 'family'. Brock understood the situation and smiled as he watched us. Riley and I finally let go of each other.

"I never thought I'd see one of those in person," I said.

"It's old school. I like it," Riley said.

"Thank you, guys, again," I said.

"You don't have to thank us," she said.

"Any time, Drew," Brock said. "Never hesitate to ask for anything."

* * *

I brought my bag into my room while Riley and Brock went to the kitchen to make breakfast. I quickly put my clothes away and didn't even bother to put the strings back into my athletic shorts or my sweatshirt. I was too excited.

I looked out of the windows to the street below and took in the aura of controlled chaos that was Manhattan. I went back to my bag and found my notebook. I laid it next to the typewriter, which I proceeded to stare at, looking to find every little piece of machinery involved and what it did. I'd never used one before. I'd only see them in movies or in pictures of famous writers from the Beat Generation. Something about typing on them seemed so pure. You watched ink get splattered onto the page in front of you as you created tangible work.

I turned to my notebook I'd put on my desk and sat in the computer chair. Flipping through the pages, I found the poem Leighton had first read. At the top of the page in the heading, I saw her phone number circled with asterisks next to it that read, "For when we get out of this place."

I chuckled to myself and pulled out my phone from my jean pocket eagerly, but I set it down on the desk and swiveled in my chair while I thought about what to do next.

I battled with my anxiety and wondered about the possible outcomes, writing premature scripts for the future, only to come to the conclusion that I couldn't do that. The image of Leighton showing me her scars crawled through my brain. I couldn't get over those. They made her seem perfect, more than she could have been without them. It's not that we were healed, we were damaged.

With that recognition, I couldn't turn down someone who would understand the certain struggles we would face adapting back into reality. I hoped she felt the same. My fingers nervously dialed the number, shaking with every digit entered. I pressed the call button and tried to hold the phone steady against my ear. The ringing sounded before I heard a girl's voice on the other end.

"Hello," she said.

"Leighton?" I asked.

"Yes," she said.

"It's Drew," I said, holding my breath.

"Drew. I'm glad you called," she said.

"I wasn't gonna leave you hanging," I said.

"It's good to hear you," she said.

"You too," I said.

The silence extended for a few seconds.

"So what's up?" she asked with a chuckle.

"Nothing much, I just got home," I said.

"How's your sister's apartment?" she asked.

"Pretty incredible," I said. "She's helping me out a lot right now."

"She sounds great," Leighton said.

"Yeah, she is," I said. "What are you up to?"

"Right now, I'm in Connecticut visiting my foster parents' friends," she said.

"Nice, how is it?" I asked.

"It's nice," she said. "But I'm happy to be heading back tomorrow morning."

"Yeah, I know what you mean. I wanted to ask you, if you're up for it tomorrow, maybe grabbing some food with me? Talk about art or something," I asked nervously.

"Talk about art?" she laughed. "Yeah, sure. I'd like that. Got any place in mind?"

"Otis told me about this place, Oscar's on 60th and Lexington. Said it was good. Does that work?" I asked.

"Yeah, that's great, I haven't been to the Upper East Side in a while," she said.

"Should I bring some writing?" I asked.

"How about you tell me why you're living in the city and we'll call it even," she said.

I thought about her words. My life with my dad was gone. I was no longer welcome into his or Pierce's world. I belonged in a different one.

"Okay, you still gonna bring some of your artwork though?" I asked.

"Yeah," she laughed.

"Okay, great. I'll call you tomorrow. Does 1:00 sound good?" I asked.

"Sounds perfect," she said.

"Great. See you then," I said.

"Bye," she said.

I hung up the phone and felt butterflies in my stomach, but they weren't the kind that I usually had to fend off. They didn't drop into the pit of my stomach and run rampant. It was nervous excitement, but the latter outweighed the former.

I smiled at myself before I looked at the blank pages stacked next to the typewriter. The keys of the typewriter seemed to beckon me forward.

I heard Leighton's voice asking to see more writing and Riley's voice telling me to never second guess myself. Granted, I never thought of myself as talented. I just enjoyed writing. But then Dr. Phillips's words came to mind and I looked back at my experience. A life rife with something that most people would never get to experience.

I turned to the typewriter and slid a piece of paper in, awkwardly fumbling the dials until only the header protruded.

"Drew, you want some food? Brock and I are making sandwiches," Riley called out.

"Sure, I'll be there in a second," I yelled back.

I rose and stood over the desk, glancing at the typewriter and then back at my wrists where I could slightly see the scar sticking out from under the fabric of my sweatshirt sleeve.

"It's all fodder," I heard Dr. Phillips say. "It's all fodder."